RAVES FOR SNOWSISTERS

"SNOWSISTERS offers a delightful and much-needed opportunity for LGBTQIA readers to find themselves starring within the pages of a novel, but the message is a universal one: We are the architects of our own stories, and we are the ones who decide when and where those stories are told. A wonderful, important debut."

—Jodi Picoult, NYT bestselling author
of *Small Great Things*

"A compelling portrayal of two young girls from different worlds headed after what they want but slowing down enough to connect and remind us that strength and doing the right thing can be all kinds of messy and complicated—I'm all over that!"

—M-E Girard, author of *Girl Mans Up*

"At the heart of this timely, well-crafted novel is a beautifully rendered relationship. Soph and Tess, different as night and day meet at a women's writing retreat in the middle of winter in the middle of nowhere. What happens between them will touch your heart, as all good stories do. A shining and promising debut."

—Sarah Weeks, author of *So B. It*

Tom Wilinsky AND Jen Sternick

interlude **press**™ • new york

For the girls who know what they want to say
(whether they say it out loud or not)
and for those who are still finding their voices.

*Snow brings a special quality with it, the power
to stop life as you know it dead in its tracks.*

—Nancy Hatch Woodward

A note for readers: Some of the characters in this book are unreliable narrators. Some have opinions and information about the world which are not well-informed. Others are subjected to that ignorance.

This book contains transphobic and homophobic language and descriptions of transphobic bullying. It also contains misgendering of a transperson and a description of violent, homophobic child abuse.

(www.interludepress.com/content-warnings)

Prologue

THE AUSTEN-BROWNING INSTITUTE FOR WOMEN IN LITERATURE

Minerva College
Devon, New Hampshire 03131

November 15, 2017

Ms. Tess Desmarais
123 Spit Brook Road
Castleton, NH 03555

Re: Annual Young Women's Writing Conference

Dear Ms. Desmarais:

The Austen-Browning Institute at Minerva College is thrilled to inform you that your application to attend this year's Young Women's Writing Conference has been approved. Since you have demonstrated a financial need, the Institute will cover fifty percent of your cost. As you know, the conference welcomes young women ages fifteen to eighteen, who show promise in writing, for a week of seminars, readings, and creative exchanges.

This year's conference will be held at Minerva's MacMorrow Artists' Retreat in Granite Notch, New Hampshire. The conference will run from February 10 through February 17. Attendees will share rooms, and each room will be assigned various tasks during the week.

We have assigned you to Room E in the main lodge. Your roommate will be **Soph. Alcazar** from **New York, New York**. You and your roommate will be responsible for **Tuesday (2/13) dinner** and **Friday (2/16) breakfast**.

Please arrange to be at the Retreat by 3:00 p.m. on Saturday, February 10, 2018. Enclosed please find a travel guide along with instructions for reimbursement of travel expenses. We also enclose a schedule of events for the conference.

Congratulations!

Very truly yours,
Helen Forsythe, Ph.D
Director

Encls.

Chapter One

*From the Fan Fiction Unbound Archive,
posted by conTessaofthecastle:*

"Daphne, are you sure this is going to work?" Astoria sounded nervous as they crept along the rapidly darkening path leading away from the Coven's fire site. They had discussed the plan last night. Daphne thought that if they could just make it past the Coriolan Woods and through the Meadow of Cymbel to the Portal of Arden, they would be able to find a spell-caster who could help them defeat the dark magic of Lord Quintana. They needed to master the space-shifting spell.

Soph.

"SOPHRONIA!"

"Coming!" Lugging my big backpack, I run down the long hallway and swing open the double doors to the kitchen. I'm holding a copy of *Q3R/F*, one of the more out-there zines, which shows a shot (probably photoshopped) of a half-naked Ellen Page on the cover. My mom sits on the high stool in her "office," which is the converted pantry. She puts down the intercom to the doormen's station and picks up a teacup, which she cradles in both hands. When the picture of Ellen catches her eye, she blinks slowly at me, which is Mom-code for counting to ten before she speaks.

She sighs and says, "Soph, one of the doormen just called. The car is here. Please don't make the Pecketts wait. Betty packed the medium-sized Vera Bradley for you. Did you check to make sure you have enough warm clothes? Have you got everything?"

"I'm fine, okay?" *I did a little packing of my own*, I think, as I jiggle my knapsack. They'll never notice that bottle of Hennessy missing from Papa's den. It was in the back of the wet bar anyway. The only other important thing is my writing journal, which has my latest poem in it, along with the stuff I scratch out every day.

"Darling, I leave it to you, but you might just tell them at the seminar that you're there for writing, not your whole life's story. And please mind your manners with the Pecketts. They are being nice enough to fly you up on their way to Bretton Woods." She really means, "Be careful about telling everyone you're gay." We've been through this before. She doesn't understand that it's completely safe for me to be out.

"Oh, puh-lease, everyone knows anyway!"

My mom says she's fine with me being gay. She just doesn't think it needs to follow me everywhere. Like I could walk out of the building and leave lesbianism in my room. Hah! I'm not changing who I am for anyone.

"Darling, I just want to make sure you're safe. I understand that you'd like to meet some other… girls, but be patient and see who they are first, all right?"

"Sure, okay." I want to get out of here as fast as I can. But she's right about how I *am* hoping I'll meet some other girls at the conference and not the jock types who go to school with me. I wish she wouldn't keep nagging me about safety, though. We're not in the 1950s or something.

Before I can escape, she reminds me, "Now, you'll be missing deportment class this week and you have to go through that before nomination and presentation next winter, so keep in mind that you have to do a special makeup in March and if anyone else is there who is also going to be presented, you must make the right impression. Genevra Peckett is on the selection committee, so she'll be voting on you and your escort next winter."

"Come on, Mom. Debutante balls are patriarchal and elitist!"

"No 'come on, Moms,' Soph. It's important to your father and me. We made a deal—you get to go to the conference in New Hampshire provided you'll cooperate and prepare for your coming out at the *Rassemblement de l'Éminent*."

"God, yes, okay." Be a debutante? I am *so* not going to do it, but I had to say I'd consider it so that they would let me go this week. Even its name smacks of privilege. When I get back, I'll put my foot down and refuse. They don't understand how wrong it is or what century we're in. Right now, I want to escape—my mother, the attitudes, the deb thing, all of it.

"And Soph, remember that Helen Forsythe is a big deal. Impress her, and you can get into any college writing program you want. Now kiss me and scoot."

I'm out the door so fast my mom probably didn't even feel my lips on her cheek, but she's usually good with an air kiss. It's true about Professor Forsythe, though; she's a big deal. I don't think I have the grades to get into her writing program, but if I impress her and take my poetry to the next level, that would definitely help. Minerva is the best school for writers!

Davey greets me in the elevator as I stuff *Q3R/F* into the top of my bag. "Where are you off to, Miss?"

"New Hampshire for the week, Davey. Big women's writing thing."

With his gloved hand, Davey holds the elevator door open for me when we reach the lobby. "Knock 'em dead, then, Miss!"

I wave at him as I rush through the door to the street without waiting for whoever is on duty to hold it for me. The big black car is waiting, and I hop in.

Tess.

SOMETIMES WHEN A CALF IS born the mother cow rejects it. No one knows why or when it will happen, but today it happened and I am standing in the small barn in the freezing cold, pouring feed over the newborn's back, which is supposed to trick her mother into licking off the placental matter, trigger her maternal hormones, and lead her to accept her own child.

Daddy is in the large barn working on a problem with the milking equipment, and I'm impatient. The work is messy and cold, and I want to go talk to Joey, who's up in the hayloft, not spend my time making things happen that are supposed to happen naturally.

The newborn calf is shivering and looks miserable. I want to clean her off and bundle her in a warm blanket, but I can't because the wet mess on her is what her mother needs to find to learn her scent. So instead I name her, even though Daddy has a rule against naming the calves before they bond with their mothers, in case it doesn't work out. I call her Angie, and, when I tell her softly what a good girl she is, how she's going to be fine, and that her mother will come over soon, she stares at me as though she believes me.

I've tried a couple of things to get her mother interested, but they didn't work, and part of me wants to give up and call Daddy to figure it out. He's under a time crunch with the evening milking coming, though, and he trusted me with Angie. I pour another scoop of feed over the calf's back.

"Don't worry," I say to Angie before I lead her mother to her side.

Once I push her nose right into the feed all over her calf, the mother does become interested. When I leave them and climb the ladder to the hayloft, Angie is nursing and her mother is letting her. I can't go too far until I'm sure the mother won't reject Angie again, but I can hear them from up here.

"It should *not* be this hard for parents to figure out how to accept their own children," I say as I flop down next to Joey in the hay. My jeans are filthy and, even though I washed my hands in the service sink, I probably smell awful.

Joey glances up from his phone, pretends to glare at me, and says, "You've met my dad, right?"

I roll my eyes at him, and he asks me again if I sent in the registration form for the writing conference.

Again, I tell him I'm still deciding. We've had this conversation at least twenty times since the letter came.

My English teacher, Mrs. Pezzuli, gave me the link for The Young Women's Writing Conference back in October. It's a week in Granite Notch, New Hampshire with two dozen other high school girls who want to write. Granite Notch is only an hour away from Castleton, in the White Mountains. I was intrigued. I mean, I never knew there were writing workshops for high school students, let alone workshops for girls. My mom used to teach high school English, and, when I showed it to her, she thought it looked pretty good but reminded me I would need a scholarship to be able to go.

Joey made me send in the application anyway and he picked the writing sample I sent, from the chapter in my fan fiction where Daphne and Astoria, the two main witches, decide that they are going to go rogue and leave their coven together. I've been working on this story for six months now and I'm up to fifty-four thousand words. It's based on that TV show, *The Witches' Circle*. In the real show's plot, Daphne has a charming blond boyfriend, and Astoria is always looking for love in all the wrong places. I prefer to focus on what they do with their magic and how they form a powerful team. I just write it for fun, to practice, and because everything you post online is anonymous. No one except Joey knows I'm the author.

Anyway, I sat on my acceptance letter for almost a month. With only a partial scholarship, I need to find two hundred and fifty dollars or I can't go.

After listening to me blather on *again* for half an hour over whether I should pay for it from the money I earned last summer scooping ice cream at the Lickety Split or save that money for after graduation as I was planning, Joey announces that I'm going and gets up to leave. Boys are like that. They just decide stuff. The cows are moving toward the milking room door. Outside, my younger sister Molly is talking to my dad as they get the equipment ready.

"I'm calling it. You're going. Hey, that's what boyfriends are for, right?" Joey scrounges through his backpack for something to write down the English homework assignment on. This always happens. He doesn't get the assignment, and I have to give it to him later. Now he has to walk home to help with the chores at his folks' place.

"I'll give you a ride up there. Dad will let me take the truck if we're on a date. You know you have to go, Tess."

I don't always like it when Joey gets bossy. I argue, not because I don't think he's right, but to prove his way of looking at it isn't the only one. I need to learn to speak up. I'm usually pretty quiet. But I plan to go into the military next year, one way or another and, from what my dad says, I'm going to need to speak up for myself. And Joey's pretty safe to practice on.

"But if I use that money, I might not have enough saved for later." I don't say what I'm thinking about being away from home for the first time.

"So?" he shrugs. "You work another job next summer, before you leave. And the military's going to pay you one way or the other. Besides, this might *help* you with the military, Tess." I hadn't thought of that. He finally locates a pen and a spiral-bound notebook and looks at me. "Tess, you're an awesome writer, even if no one knows you. It's time to tell people who you are." He's smiling at me, but I'm still nervous.

"Fine," I sigh. "Pages three hundred to three-twenty-five of *Of Mice and Men*, and there's going to be a vocab quiz on the words she put on the board."

He scribbles it down, zips up his pack, and says, "Email me the words after dinner, please?" Then he drops a kiss on my head and swings himself around to go down the ladder.

"Hey, Joey?" I say, as he peers down to see the rungs. He looks up. I want to tell him I'm nervous to be going to a conference with a bunch of girls from all over, but I stop myself. I'm leaving Castleton one way or the other after graduation. Joey and I promised each other that. He's right. I need to practice.

"Be careful getting home in the dark," I tell him. He grins at me. His jaw is still a little crooked from when it was broken last fall and they set it wrong. It makes his smile slightly lopsided. He shrugs and heads down the ladder.

I hear Daddy calling me from below. His voice is sharp. "Tess? Why didn't you take care of this calf?" When I get down the ladder, Joey is disappearing out the door after quickly greeting my father. Daddy is struggling with Angie's mother, who is kicking at Angie.

"You know better than this, Tess," says Daddy, struggling to get to Angie while her mother thrashes. "You know not to walk away before a job is done."

I wince as a hoof hits Angie and knocks her off her wobbly legs before Daddy can intervene. Angie's brown eyes follow me as I rush to help Daddy with the restraints.

✳ ✳ ✳

From Soph Alcazar's Writing Journal,
February 10, 2018

From the City to cold, mountains, and snow,
For new blood, openness, I am ready
To write, meet, show what I already know:
That we all should be out, proud and steady.

And learn how to write in a new structure.
Something advanced, a shape I've never done.
Edge of the new; am I at a juncture?
Hoping also that I find a someone.

So far, there's been no one, but I'm sixteen.
My parents desperate that I conform.
They don't understand it's me they demean.
I won't dance their steps however they storm.

Because I know who I am. I won't change.
No matter if they insist, 'not their page.

Chapter Two

From the Fan Fiction Unbound Archive,
posted by conTessaofthecastle:

Daphne wasn't sure at all, but she didn't want Astoria to know her fears. She stopped in the path and waited for Astoria, so close she could turn, look into her dark eyes, and smell the scent of roses mixed with ash that always clung to her. When she spoke, it was barely a whisper. "We're going to be fine. As long as we stay together, we're going to be fine." Astoria looked at her and shuddered.

Soph.

MRS. PECKETT IS ONE OF those mothers who always has an agenda. I'm not complaining, though. They were nice to let me tag along on their plane and I think their son Freddy and I may have more in common than any of our parents realize. Freddy's a year behind me in school, a sophomore. He goes to an all-boys' school, St. Botolph's, so I only see him when our mothers arrange something that puts us in the same room. He's quiet, wears glasses, and avoids sports, which makes me wonder what he's going to do while his parents are skiing this week. A blue streak in his hair makes me smile. It's pretty fly, but that won't thrill his parents. They're retro in the bad way, not cool but conservative, as if they get all their information from newspapers and cocktail parties.

Back when we went to elementary school, Freddy was one of those boys who liked to play with girls more than boys, and we were good friends. While the other boys played with Legos and *Star Wars* figures, Freddy played with Barbies and he did it well, imagining all sorts of stories we acted out with the dolls. My friend Lally had a big set and all the accessories, cars, and the doctor's office, and we used to make playdates with Freddy at her apartment. Lally told all the other girls about it one day, and those playdates ended pretty quickly. Freddy became a lot less talkative after that and now I only see him when our families get together. On those occasions, he's usually buried in a phone or a laptop.

I wonder if Freddy's gay. But he's never said anything to anyone we know. I have no patience for the closet. If he's gay, he should come out. Coming out is better for everyone.

Mr. Peckett sits in the far corner of the airplane cabin hidden behind his *Wall Street Journal Weekend Edition*. He must be the last person alive who still reads the paper version.

Mrs. Peckett sits next to me and wastes no time. "Sophronia, it's lovely to fly you up with us, right, Freddy?" Freddy, across the table from me, barely looks up from his iPad. He nods at his mother and me. "Norris and I understand this is going to be your debutante year. And with your family background, you must be very excited!"

I'm excited all right, but not about that. "Oh, that's a long way off, Mrs. P. Not 'til next winter."

"Nonsense, we know all that advance preparation starts now. You have to take ballroom dancing and pick your charity. Have you thought about your escort? Your parents are not going to want you to be presented on the arm of a young man you've never met from one of the military academies, are they? If you don't have a special young man of your own, wouldn't you prefer to have a family friend?"

She's thinking about Freddy, of course, who is still looking at his screen. I like him well enough for a "family friend," but we have almost nothing in common anymore and he's so quiet most of the time that I want to yell at him to say something. He still doesn't move from his iPad, so I can't see his face, but I get the feeling he's concentrating on ignoring us a little too much. My mom was pretty clear about not discussing being a lesbian and, even though I think it's bullshit to keep quiet about it, I do. But since I'm out to everybody, Freddy must know, from the few times we've hung out together, that there isn't going to be any "special young man." I wish he'd help me out. "Escort?" I reply. "Oh, no. Not yet."

Mrs. Peckett turns back to me and chirps, "Well, don't wait too long. The good ones may be taken!"

I smile and take out my phone. "I'll be careful, Mrs. P. Promise!" What else am I going to say? "No f-ing way am I doing it at all?" "For an escort, I'm thinking maybe a hot biker chick?" Instead, I ask, "Is it okay to use my phone now that we're in flight?"

Freddy finally looks up. "Yeah, the Wi-Fi code is NorrisJPeckett3, no spaces. The Arabic three, not the Roman numerals Dad uses in his signature." The real Norris J. Peckett, III, shuffles his newspaper.

As soon as I turn my phone on, I find a text.

[FROM FREDDY TO SOPH] *Sorry! Just agree with her, and she'll shut up.*

Maybe Freddy is cooler than I thought.

[FROM SOPH TO FREDDY] *K. My parents are all over me about this.*

Freddy catches my eye across the table and smiles at me.

I send my friend Gordon an update.

[FROM SOPH TO GORDON] *On plane. Freddy's mom trying to make him my deb-escort!!!*

Gordon met Freddy when their mothers signed them up for indoor sports at the armory years ago—a disaster for both of them—but we don't all hang out together. Gordon also thinks Freddy is gay, but that he's too shy to tell anyone.

Gordon texts back a few minutes later.

[FROM GORDON TO SOPH] *If U don't want Freddy, I get him!*

This is getting good quickly. I add two other friends, Lally and Mibs, to the chat.

[FROM SOPH TO GORDON, LALLY, AND MIBS] *He dyed his hair blue.*

Gordon responds immediately.

[FROM GORDON TO LALLY, MIBS, AND SOPH] *I can make it work!*

The four of us go to a prep school in the City. Gordon is the only boy in our class who's out.

Lally chimes in.

[FROM LALLY TO GORDON, MIBS, AND SOPH] *S—stop. New Hampshire is to get into college. G can get his own dates.*

I laugh at that. Lally sometimes makes fun of the rest of us for being too obsessed with finding someone we can fall in love with, but she's right. Minerva College is my dream college, a traditional small school set in a picture-perfect historic New England town. I imagine ivy-covered brick buildings and a quad littered with maple trees. I would be far away from my mother. I love the great creative writing program, but it only takes top students. I need to impress Professor Forsythe. She's not only the director of this conference, she's also the chair of the English Department at Minerva. Mibs doesn't answer any of us, which is no big surprise, since she's been busy with her new boyfriend for weeks now. I sign off the text and google Professor Helen Forsythe. I have one week to convince her I'm the perfect candidate for Minerva. I need to find out everything about her, because I can't mess this up.

Tess.

I GET UP AT FIVE in the morning and spend the morning packing and repacking my dad's army duffel bag. I've never been away from home for a week, and I check six times that I packed enough warm socks and underwear. I don't own a laptop computer; we just have the desktop in the family room that we share, so I make sure to bring a couple of spiral-bound notebooks and a bunch of pens and pencils. At least I got a phone for Christmas this year, so I can do research on that. My knapsack is already pretty full when I go to the computer and pull up my bookmarked tabs. I hesitate and then I click open a few pages and print them out. I look over all the questions as they emerge from the printer, but my eyes come back to the one I always get stuck on. *Describe a recent incident where you took the lead.* I stuff the papers in my knapsack. I only have two more weeks to figure out how to respond to that. Or, you know, actually find a way to *take the lead.* Joey's truck pulls in the driveway, and I go to find Mom and Daddy to say goodbye.

On my way out, I stop in the small barn. Molly is there, giving a bottle to Angie. We never could get her mother to let her nurse. I took over the bottle-feeding and I offered to not go to the writing conference, but Daddy sighed and told me he knew I was leaving next year anyway and Molly could handle it while I was gone. I didn't dare tell him I had named her too. The barn is cold. I tell Molly goodbye and that I'm sorry about leaving her with all the work. She shrugs, smiles, and tells me to enjoy myself at the conference. Angie ignores me. She's focused on the milk.

I'm quiet in the truck as Joey and I drive to Granite Notch. Joey turns the radio off and peers sideways at me. "What?" he says, looking back at the road. Part of me loves that Joey always gets me.

"I'm just…"

He waits for me to finish my sentence. When I don't, he takes one hand off the steering wheel and pats my thigh.

"It'll be fine, Tess. Your story is great, and now you get the chance to see what you can do outside of Castleton, New Hampshire. You haven't given up on that, have you?"

We've been talking about how to get out of Castleton since we started high school. In the last year, since he broke his jaw and we've been seniors, leaving is pretty much *all* we talk about.

"Fine," I say. His hand is heavy on my thigh. "We'll see how I do an hour away from home in *Granite Notch*, New Hampshire. It isn't a big chance, Joey."

"Yes, it is, Tess!" He takes his hand back to adjust the steering wheel. "It's a *really* big chance for you. You're just as good as those other girls, or they wouldn't have picked you. Minerva College is a big deal. Once you show them who you are, they'll respect you. Think of it as basic training for Basic Training. You know, living with a bunch of strange girls and getting compared to them, like all that stuff you're going to be doing next year."

"*Show them who I am*? Seriously, Joey? That's the best pep talk you can come up with?" I grin at him and roll my eyes, but, despite the sarcasm in my voice, I understand what he means. I'm headed into the military next year one way or the other. That means lots of new people and places and situations. This probably *is* a good time to practice. The interview prompt on the paper in my knapsack runs through my head. *Describe a recent incident where you took the lead.* I don't know about being a leader. I only know I'm number three in my high school class, my latest fan fiction got more than thirty thousand hits, and I absolutely, positively have to leave Castleton. The military interview scheduled in two weeks is my best chance. Somehow, I have to figure out how this writing workshop might help. I take a breath and think about what Daddy said before I left the house. "Tess, make us proud now." He was focused on finding something in his toolbox when he said it, though.

We pull up to the lodge where the conference is, and Joey hops out of the truck to say goodbye. I have the duffel bag slung over one shoulder and my knapsack, stuffed with notebooks and papers, in my hand.

I must look scared because Joey gives me a quick hug and says into my ear, "Try to be yourself, Tess, and text me sometime. I want to hear all about the other girls." Then he winks and gets into the truck. I take a deep breath, think that the last thing I'm going to be for the next week is myself, and go into the lobby.

✳ ✳ ✳

From Soph Alcazar's Writing Journal,
February 10, 2018

Query: what is this really all about:
Minerva, my sonnets, just getting out?
Or could I find someone, perfect for me,
Not secretive, but out there, she will be.

Chapter Three

From the Fan Fiction Unbound Archive,
posted by conTessaofthecastle:

The two of them made camp in silence. They worked
efficiently, each anticipating the other's motions and each
moving around the other comfortably. Astoria cleared a space
for a campfire and unpacked some bread and cheese for their
supper. Meanwhile, Daphne collected firewood and made
note of the nearest stream for water. It wasn't until the fire
was built and they sat watching the flames that Astoria asked,
"What happens if we fail?"

Soph.

I'M LATE, OF COURSE, BUT it's not my fault. The little airport in
New Hampshire is all jammed up because a big snowstorm is
coming, and private planes don't have priority. After I air-kiss
the Pecketts, Freddy smacks his lips suggestively in my ear and
actually winks at me, as if he's up to something.

I immediately text Gordon.

[FROM SOPH TO GORDON] *F may be a better prospect 4 U than*
I thought—he vamped it up with a wink and a kiss!

Gordon responds by repeating himself.

[FROM GORDON TO SOPH] *If U don't want him, I get him.*

Then I discover that I was wrong to expect a line of yellow taxicabs waiting at the arrivals area. Google to the rescue, but there's no Uber up here and it takes almost an hour to find someone from the local taxi company to pick me up, so it's after three o'clock when I finally arrive at the MacMorrow Retreat. The sky is overcast, and the weather is getting colder. The cab driver tells me they expect ten inches of snow to fall tonight. I imagined something more Adirondack-style, with pitched roofs and porches on each level, but this is a basic ski lodge: a single, squat, three-story brick building up a long, wooded driveway. I'm disappointed that the retreat is not on the Minerva campus, but I've never been closer before, so who cares? Excited to be here, I bound up the few stairs to the entrance.

The lobby is tiny and marked by a card table with balloons over it. Phew, at least there are a few girls as late as me waiting to sign in. I stand at the back of the line, behind a tall, long-limbed girl with beautiful dark brown, shoulder-length hair pulled back with a thick cloth headband. She turns around when I stand behind her.

"Hi, I'm Soph."

"Orly Erwin," she says in a soft, low voice. She's wearing dangly gold earrings which hang almost to her shoulders.

"Great to meet you. I was afraid I'd be the last one." I can't help checking her out. After all, I'm already a junior in high school but still have no experience. You'd think in New York I'd be able to meet someone, but only Mibs did. Gordon says, "The bigger the pond, the fewer the fish worth looking at."

There aren't even any other lesbians on the literary magazine at school. Lally, who fences, claims that the only other ones are on the field hockey team and we have nothing to say to each other. Anyway, Orly is decent looking, very put-together, a little too hair-and-makeup for my taste. She's in loose purple harem-y pants and a heavy purple sweater—like something you'd see on an old TV show, fluffy, with a high collar—under a lightweight maroon coat. She coordinated the color of her headband with her coat.

Orly smiles a little, as if she's shy, and says, "You *are* the last one in. But the van from Boston was very late, and I think Joan here is ready to get out from behind her table." Her voice is friendly, and she has a Southern accent, warm and welcoming. She steps back, revealing Joan, a frowning woman with glasses who is seated at the table, handling registration.

"Hello, you're the twenty-fourth, Sophie Al-CAY-sah." Her tone is flat, as though she doesn't care if I'm Gertrude Stein herself.

"Yes. It's Soph. Al-cah-ZAR." I don't mind if people screw up my last name—which is shortened from Dad's super-long one that never fits on any form—but I am *not* a Sophie.

"Yes, Soph. Room E. You're sharing with Tess, next to Orly and Chris. On the second floor. Go up the stairs over there." She hands us both old-fashioned brass room keys on tags and nametags in clear plastic. Mine says "Sophie."

Orly and I grab our luggage. Joan calls after us, "Don't forget the Mocktail Party at five p.m." As we climb the stairs, I notice that we're both carrying floral-print, quilted duffels from Vera Bradley. "You too, huh? My mom loves this flowery stuff."

Orly says, "Huh? You mean my 'Tar-zhay' special?" She smiles a little.

"Oh, um, yeah," I say without understanding what she means.

"Isn't it cute? I have a matching makeup bag to go with it." She holds up her other hand and, sure enough, she's carrying a smaller matching bag.

"Neat," I say as we reach the second floor. I don't wear much makeup, but whatever. "Where are you from, Orly?"

Orly pauses. Avoiding my eyes, she says, "Georgia. You?"

"New York."

Orly gets to her room first. "Soph, darlin', will you hold my makeup bag for me?" She hands the bag to me and fumbles for her key.

Before she has a chance to use her key, the door opens, and a girl our age stands in the doorway. She's very short, probably less than five feet tall, and sturdily built with short, jet black hair and black, plastic-rimmed glasses. She's barefoot and wearing a pair of worn jeans and a navy-blue fleece pullover. She's staring intently at us.

"Hi. I'm Chris. You can't both be Orly." She says it without smiling.

Orly is frozen; she doesn't say anything, just looks at me, eyes wide. I say, "No, I'm Soph. This is Orly. I'm in the room next door." I'm not waiting around for them to figure out what to say to each other, so I hand Orly her makeup bag. As Orly goes in and closes the door behind her, I stroll over to Room E.

I knock, figuring that I might as well warn my roommate in case she's all abrupt like Chris. I can hear someone in the room talking and then footsteps. The door opens to reveal a girl my height with long, straight, dark blonde hair. She is wearing a pink sweater, shell pink polish coats her fingernails and—oh, brother—a charm bracelet encircles her left wrist, one of those

Pandora things that went out about five years ago. I had one in sixth grade. All the charms on it are either silver or set with pink stones. I notice hot pink fuzzy socks on her feet. I haven't seen this much pink since elementary school. I almost feel as if I'm meeting Barbie in real life—or My Little Pony. She holds a cell phone to her chest.

I push into the room past her, since my bag is getting heavy, and say, "Hi, Tess, right? I'm sorry I'm late."

Tess puts up a finger, turns around and says into her phone, "Hey, Joey, I've gotta go now. Things are starting up." After a pause, she says, in a voice I can barely hear, "Yes, yes, you're a great boyfriend. Be good while I'm gone, okay?" Then she puts her phone down and turns to me. Butterflies flutter in my chest. She's obviously a girly-girl and crazy about her boyfriend. I should be able to respect that.

"Hi, Soph, right? Or is it Sophia or something?" I fiddle with my bag, put it on the bed, and then move it to the floor. When I look up at her again, I notice her eyes. They're blue, but with flecks of green. I've never seen anyone with eyes that color. Too bad about the boyfriend.

"Just Soph, short for Sophronia. Definitely not Sophie."

"It's pretty. I never heard of it. Is it Russian or something?"

I get this a lot. "Nope, Greek by way of Spain. Sophronia is a family name. My dad's family is Spanish. My full last name is Borbón del Alcazar. But it got shortened, for obvious reasons."

"Ah."

Tess seems puzzled, but doesn't add anything. I babble, which I always do when I'm nervous. "Dad's family is Spanish, but they got booted in the Civil War. You know, Franco made it a monarchy again, but he didn't want anyone to challenge him, just Juan Carlos at the end."

"Juan Carlos at the end? But I thought the Civil War ended somewhere in Virginia…"

I try to rein myself in. "Oh, well, yeah. So where are you from? Desmarais sounds French."

Tess blinks at me. "Ummm, it's pronounced *Dess-mare-iss*, not *Day-mah-ray*. I'm from nearby, Castleton, New Hampshire, in the next county over. My name is French-Canadian. I don't think anyone's been worried about us challenging the king lately."

Embarrassed, I change topics. "I'm here to work on poetry. How about you?"

"I want to learn as much as I can. I still can't believe this kind of workshop exists, and that they accepted me. Someday I want to write a whole novel, but the piece I sent in is part of a story I write online." She pauses. Her next sentence comes out slowly. "It's fan fiction."

"Oh yeah, I've read some of that." It surprises me that fan fiction impressed Professor Forsythe enough to let her in. My guidance counselor suggested I apply to this workshop to boost my college applications. Everyone at my school is flying around the country this spring, doing special "invited" group activities like Mock United Nations and Junior Theater Festival to increase their admissions chances. Don't people outside the City do that too? I mean, I read some fan fiction every now and then, and I like it, but people are snobby about it. I wonder if this workshop will be serious enough to include on my applications.

I ask, "Fan of what?"

Tess hesitates, then answers, "*The Witches' Circle*. You know, the television show?"

I don't know it, so I nod and change the subject.

Tess

I PULL ON MY LOAFERS just before five o'clock so we can go to the Mocktail Party. Soph's arrival has made it a little awkward, more than a little awkward. Everything she says and does leaves me feeling sort of diminished, as though I shrink an inch or two every time she mentions something casually that I've never heard of. The whole explanation about her name is confusing but apparently I'm supposed to know who her family is.

She plops her bag down and pulls stuff out, making a pile of clothes on the floor by her bed. She takes out a black pen and pulls her name tag apart so she can delete the "ie" they added to the end of her name.

Soph is from New York—the real city part, Manhattan. She lives in an apartment and took a private plane to get here, which is why she's late. I've never ridden on a plane. She's wearing dark-wash skinny jeans pushed into black suede boots, which the snow is going to ruin, and a soft black wool sweater with an asymmetrical neckline. She's got sparkly studs in her ears that may be real diamonds, but not chips. They're, like, the size of peas. Also, she talks almost nonstop from the time she arrives until we go downstairs. My mom would call her a "Chatty Cathy." I've never met anyone like her. I mean, I know that was the point of coming to this whole workshop, but I'm still figuring out how to act.

She tells me about going to a private school near her house. I ask her if she walks to school, and she says, "Yeah, everyone walks to school together."

She tells me that she writes poetry. I don't know much about poetry. I've read some, obviously, in school, but it seems hard to write, as though you need to spill your innermost secrets out on paper in fragmented sentences and make them rhyme, either that or write about nature, like Robert Frost. I'm not really sure how any of that works, but I figure she must be good if she's here.

She went to the Caribbean over Christmas with her family, to a resort on Saint something—I didn't recognize him. When she asks me if I ever go to the islands, I shake my head no.

"We can't leave the herd to go on vacation," I tell her, before I realize what I'm saying. Oh. My. God. I am *such* a loser.

She purses her lips and asks, "You mean your posse?"

We're from different planets, and now I need to spill it, even as I shrink another two inches. "I live on a dairy farm," I admit. "We raise cows." Once I say that, she actually stops talking. She looks at me through these long, dark eyelashes and just blinks a couple of times.

I'm pretty nervous after all this, so I text Joey to reassure me, but I don't get an answer. Then I google some of what Soph told me about her family on my phone so I won't sound so uninformed later. Unfortunately, that makes me feel smaller, because it turns out her family used to be royalty in Spain. Great. The first time I dare to go away from home, and I end up rooming with a real princess. I feel like Cinderella. Before the ball.

When we get down to the lounge where the party is, all the other girls are already there. A tall girl with a name tag that reads "Orly" comes over to Soph, and Soph introduces us.

"Orly, this is my roommate, Tess. Orly was in line just ahead of me when I got here."

"Hi, Orly. Where are you coming from?"

"From outside Atlanta. It's never this cold at home!" She has a soft voice and she speaks slowly. I guess it's her accent, but she sounds friendly. I can't believe people came for this workshop from so far away.

"You get used to it. I'm from nearby, well, an hour away."

Orly raises her eyebrows. "Don't tell me it's north of here and even colder?"

We laugh, and then Orly's roommate Chris comes over. Chris is short and kind of loud. She makes me nervous the way Soph does, even though they aren't the same at all.

Chris is from Dallas, Texas. She goes to a charter school and she says she is a journalist for her school newspaper. Not a reporter or a writer—a *journalist*. I hope Soph doesn't mention the herd to her.

"I'm also working on a longer investigative piece about misogyny toward high school athletes which I intend to submit to the Times." I guess she means the *New York Times*, but I don't want to ask. The shrinking feeling comes over me again. Some of the other girls introduce themselves. Janaye is from New York too, someplace near Manhattan. She writes fiction, like me. She's talkative like Soph and they chat about a new band they both know; they pull out their phones to find a video, but the cell reception is bad up here.

"I guess we're not in Kansas anymore, huh, Janaye?" asks Soph, with wide, excited eyes. Janaye laughs with her. I cringe, but I don't think they notice. Orly goes to ask Joan, the organizer, about something, and Chris turns to me with a fixed glare. She's about three inches shorter than I am, but I feel as though she's taller. I sip at my Sprite, hoping I won't say something stupid, when suddenly she hisses in my ear.

"Two things."

I'm not sure if she is asking me a question or making an announcement. She's right up close to me, her short, dark hair is gelled up straight off her head, and I can smell something herby, the way the kitchen smells when Mom roasts a chicken. I want to back up, but before I can, she speaks again. I guess she's making an announcement after all.

"One: They let writers in who write *fan fiction*, for fuck's sake. What kind of a joke is that?" I hold my breath. I can feel my face turning red. I want to leave this room so much. But Chris isn't done.

"And two: My roommate's really a guy."

✳ ✳ ✳

From Soph Alcazar's Writing Journal,
February 10, 2018

I try with second and first, roommate, friend?
But despite our efforts, none comprehends.
So recall, Soph, concentrate on being
Here. What's important is your succeeding.

Chapter Four

From the Fan Fiction Unbound Archive,
posted by conTessaofthecastle:

> In the morning, Daphne stretched and rose stiffly from
> the hard ground they had slept on. She heard Astoria singing
> softly to herself. She watched as Astoria secured her blanket
> around their food and started to cover the ashes from the fire
> last night. Her golden hair fell over her face as she worked.
> Daphne recognized the song she was singing. It was a child's
> play-song, one from the schoolyard.

Soph.

I MEET SOME INTERESTING GIRLS at the Mocktail Party, but everyone acts a little stiff and uncomfortable. Are they competitive? Shy? A funny sort of tension fills the room. I find Orly and introduce her to Tess. Janaye, from Brooklyn is super-cool, which is to be expected. Everyone I know from Brooklyn is a hipster, and I wanted to go to high school there, but my mother said that all the girls in her family went to Partridge and that ended that. Janaye, of course, goes to one of those artsy little schools that was bound to send someone to this conference. I bet Janaye's parents don't bug her about being presented or anything. Brooklyn is so much easier than Manhattan. When I look around, Tess is talking to

Orly's roommate, Chris, on the other side of the room. I consider going over there, but then they open the dining hall for dinner.

The dining room is set up with two long tables. A picture window has a view of a snow-filled expanse that must be a garden in the summer. Each place has a card assigning an attendee. I am seated about halfway down, between Clover from Philadelphia and Gabriela from Hartford, Connecticut, both of whom say hi, but nothing else. Joan sits at the head of one table, and Professor Forsythe stands at the head of the other. I recognize her from my google searches: a tall woman with white hair. Younger women sit at the foot of each table. Once we are all seated, Professor Forsythe clears her throat and asks for our attention.

"Good evening, everyone. I met some of you already, but for those I haven't met, I'm Helen Forsythe. I'm the director of the Austen-Browning Institute and an English professor at Minerva College. Most of my scholarly work has been in poetry. I think you've all met my colleague, Joan Cambiabrazos, who is a writing instructor at Minerva." She gestures toward Joan. "We also have with us Celestine Gross, a teaching assistant in the creative writing program at Minerva and Grace Koh, an alum of this very conference." She points at Celestine, a curly-haired brunette with glasses, who nods back, and then at Grace, a petite Asian woman, who smiles. "Grace is also your Resident Assistant. She'll be on the floor with all of you and is your go-to person for questions about the lodge."

"Welcome to the Young Women's Writing Conference! You were all selected based on your writing samples and your different backgrounds. We've also worked hard to select a group whose members have something say to each other through their writing.

During your short time here, we want you to create and share your works. We also want you to get to know each other. You are a select, but diverse, group, and this is a special opportunity for you to learn from each other. Friendships made this weekend can last a lifetime and, as a writer myself, I can tell you that there is nothing as valuable as someone who understands what you are trying to write and who can therefore react to your writing in a positive and dynamic manner."

We all clap politely, and Professor Forsythe sits down. I'm too far down the table to introduce myself to her, but I will later on. She's talking to Orly and her roommate, and I wish I could switch places with one of them. But I'm here for the week, which gives me plenty of time to impress her. We are served dinner, which is not very good, a plain baked chicken breast with white rice and a pale salad. I remember that we are all supposed to be responsible for a meal, and I wonder why the girls on duty didn't order something better.

I turn to the people next to me. Gabriela's still not very talkative, though she tells me she started writing poetry last year when her lifelong best friend went off to college. She's an artist and loves to draw. Clover is more my speed: pretty, blonde, and a little butch. She's got more of an edge than Gabriela, and I make jokes, which she laughs at. She wants to write graphic novels, and when she hears that Gabriela draws she leans forward to talk to her while I sit back.

After "dessert," which is a cold brownie and berries, Professor Forsythe stands up again. "We'll expect you back here for breakfast at eight a.m. sharp. But before you go, Grace has a short activity planned. Please clear your places and put your dishes on the counter in the kitchen. We'll see you in the lounge in a few minutes."

This is probably as good a time as any, so I walk quickly over to Professor Forsythe. "Hi Professor, I'm Soph Alcazar. From New York."

Professor Forsythe looks at me blankly. "Hello. Welcome."

"Thank you. Can I take this for you?" I lift her plate and pile the silverware on it.

"Oh. That's quite unnecessary. But, I suppose … fine. Thank you." She frowns. I just made my first mistake.

"No problem." I don't know what else to say, so I turn toward the kitchen.

"Ah, well, you know, the glass, too? And please clear your own place."

I hear the edge in her voice. Did I blow it? "Of course. Sorry." She doesn't respond.

In the lounge, Grace stands on a chair in front of the fireplace on one side of the room. "Hi, everyone. I'm Grace. We're going to play a game called 'Sorts and Mingle.' It's a way for us to learn about each other." Girls are still talking so she claps her hands twice. "Can everyone hear me?"

Everyone murmurs a general assent. Grace may be small, but her voice is clear and enthusiastic.

"I'm dividing the room into the points of a compass. I'm at the back, which is south. North is the front, which leads to the entrance to the lodge and the hallway to the conference rooms. East is to my right, where the doors to the dining room are. That leaves west, which is to my left, toward the sliding doors to the courtyard. There, now you have your map for tonight and you know where everything will take place for the rest of the week!" She smiles, as if she's said something very clever. "For the first half of the game, 'Sorts,' I'm going to call out some choices, all in pairs, and tell you to go in one direction. You have to decide between the two choices, no in-betweens. See who goes with you and who doesn't. We'll get to 'Mingle' later. Are there any questions?"

None of us asks any questions. Everyone is avoiding eye contact. I want to make a joke, but it wouldn't be nice, so I don't.

"Here we go. Urban? Go north," she points to the wall she's facing. "Rural, come south." She points to herself.

Easy. I go north, away from Grace. Janaye does too and Chris and plenty of others. Tess goes south with about a third of the girls. Orly can't decide at first, but ends up going north.

Before I can meet the other "urbans," Grace calls out, "Now, fruit go west, nuts go east." She points again as though we might be confused. But if you live in New York, you know north, south, east, and west without thinking.

Still, I'm not sure which way to go, though I know we have to choose. Gordon suffers from one of those terrible allergies, and, since I don't, I go east for the nuts. Tess is there too, and I wonder how she chose. She seems like a strawberry, sweet but also tart at the top where it's less pink. But then she nods at me, and I think maybe she's here because she's a hard nut to crack.

"Silver, south. Gold, north."

Tess freezes, but then walks toward Grace. I figure gold. I mean, we do live on Park, and it is Manhattan.

Orly comes over too, and I smile at her.

She says, "Gold complements my skin."

We split up when Grace calls out, "Fire go east; water go west." Orly, Tess, and Yin go toward the doors to the courtyard while I stand with Chris.

I don't understand where this is getting us until "Introverts east, extroverts west!" I'm almost alone now on the west with Janaye and a girl named Peggy. I guess most writers are introverted.

"One last time, comedy come to the south, tragedy go to the north."

This puts Orly, Tess, and me together on the north side. Tess looks at me quizzically but doesn't say anything. Does she think I write comic poetry? Limericks?

Grace ends the "Sorts" game and explains the "Mingle." "No more either-or, and we'll put away our compasses. Now I'm going to throw out some general questions, and you have to find others with similar answers. When you do, stand with them. Chat if you like. It doesn't matter if you stand alone. When I see people stop moving, I'll ask for the answers so everyone will know. First round, what is your favorite pie?"

Now this should be fun. Mine is key lime. Tess stands near me, so I ask her. No match. She's an apple pie girl, which is an easy group for her to find. I wonder if they're all the people who went north for "rural." Before I know it, I'm standing there alone, the only one.

Orly calls out to me from where she stands with two other girls, "Pecan pie, Soph. You can't beat it!"

I make a face. "It's too sweet for me."

From her chair, Grace goes through the groups. Apple is the biggest, not surprisingly. "You're all alone there," she calls to me. "What's your pie of choice?"

When I say, "Key lime," Chris walks around another group and joins me. Who knew? I smile at her, but she's too serious to smile back.

"What's your favorite color to wear?"

Chris stays by my side, and we pick up other "urbans" by choosing black. Now Tess is all alone. I'm surprised, since you'd think with all the girls here, pink would be popular. But then Orly joins her. I never do hear them say pink, though, because Janaye and I compare notes about our favorite designers while Grace asks everyone their colors.

Grace calls out the next question: "What do you write?"

It takes a few minutes for us to "mingle" on this one. I walk around saying "Poetry?" and end up with a few girls.

One of them, Yin, says she blogs and sometimes puts up poetry. "That's how Helen found me. She saw my blog and invited me to apply."

"Helen?"

"Yes, Helen Forsythe. The director. I hadn't even heard of this program until I got her email inviting me to apply. She's pretty cool."

"Oh, yes, Helen, of course." I try to sound "cool" like "Helen" and pretend I'm more interested in "mingling" than in why Professor Forsythe was so interested in Yin.

We go through a few other topics, like favorite movies and celebrities we most want to meet, but I found "Sorts" more fun. "Mingle" should put people together, but more people end up standing alone. Also, it happens too fast for me to learn much about any of them.

I'm relieved when Grace announces that it's nine o'clock and we should all go to bed because tomorrow is a busy day. On my way up to our bedroom, I think about how I'd better focus if I'm going to be on a first name basis with Professor Forsythe like Yin.

I linger in the hallway outside our room, talking to Janaye and some others, asking them about how they got here. No one else refers to "Helen." They all say they found out about the conference through school. Orly goes into the room next to ours. She's there for a few minutes before Chris follows. They haven't talked all night, from what I can tell. Maybe everyone is still shy about rooming with new people. I feel good about this week. Nobody here expects me to keep quiet about myself or serve as ambassador for my family. I still have six days to impress Professor Forsythe. Tomorrow I can pull out some of my work to show her. It shouldn't be hard to be friendly with everyone here, and those two things together might convince her I'm Minerva material.

Tess.

SOPH IS STILL CHATTING IN the lounge with Janaye, so I'm the first one back to our room. I don't know what to think about what Chris said to me and I can't get it out of my head. If I were braver, I would have told her I write fan fiction and asked what her problem with it was. And I don't know what I was supposed to say about Orly. I talked with Orly during "Sorts" and "Mingle," and she seems like the other girls to me. We like a lot of the same things. Her hair is long, and she wears a skirt, a yellow scarf, and dangly earrings.

Sighing, I unlock our door and scrub my face. Going through my nighttime routine might help me think. Maybe I can ask Soph about it when she gets back. I wash my face and brush my teeth, grateful for the sink in the room. I'm doing sit-ups in my pajamas when Soph comes flying through the door.

She stops short when she sees me on the floor, then laughs as she closes the door and says, "I love your PJs! Way to subvert the military-industrial complex with color!" Her laugh is distinctive, sort of glittery.

I sit up straight, confused. "Way to what?" I don't understand what she just said at all.

She pulls off her fancy suede boots, stumbles backward onto her bed, and shrugs. "I think it's great that you appropriated camouflage and asserted your femininity by making it pink. Robbing the male-dominated military culture of its aggression!"

I look down at the pajamas. "I got them for Christmas from my grandmother."

"You did?" Her eyes widen as she pushes the second boot off her foot. "Is your grandmother a feminist? That's so cool!"

I think of MeMe, leaving church before coffee hour every Sunday so she can get home to put the roast in the oven and have it ready when we all arrive for lunch, hanging laundry on the line in the summer heat, and braiding my sister's hair. I remember how she taught me to knit. It makes me smile. "No, she's probably not a feminist. She's a pretty hard worker though. She gave me these because I'm going into the military."

That should at least impress Soph a little more than being from a dairy farm.

She stops short, her arms halfway out of the sweater she's pulling off, and looks at me as though she's seeing a ghost.

"You're *what?*" she asks, even though I'm pretty sure she heard me.

"I'm going into the military. Next summer after I graduate."

"You're kidding. Why would you—" She stops as she did when I mentioned *The Witches' Circle*.

"Why would I enlist?" I can't understand why she's asking, but I explain anyway. "My family is a service family. My grandpa fought in Vietnam and my father fought in the first Iraq war. We all serve. And the military is a great place for women these days. There are opportunities for travel and job training. They'll pay for my education, one way or another."

She shakes her head at me, as though she's still confused. "Did some recruiter tell you that, Tess? Because you know they promise you things that aren't true. I don't know why you would want to do that unless you got drafted. I mean, men use war and violence to kill each other, but women can get things done without bloodshed."

Now I'm both tired and angry. Joey was wrong. Showing these girls who I am is just making them judge me. I can't ask Soph about Chris and Orly. I shouldn't have left Castleton. At least I know what's expected there. I abandon the rest of my sit-ups and climb into bed without saying anything more. I have no idea how I'm going to make it through a week of this place.

✳ ✳ ✳

From Soph Alcazar's Writing Journal
February 10, 2018

I can't understand what's going on here.
Try, fail with Forsythe; Tess in combat gear.

Chapter Five

From the Fan Fiction Unbound Archive,
posted by conTessaofthecastle:

Daphne concentrated. She closed her eyes and repeated the incantation slowly, focusing her attention on the tingling sensation in her fingertips. "Actessar," she murmured. Then again, "Actessar." For a moment, she could feel her fingers twitching and she thought she might have mastered the space-shifting spell at last. But when she opened her eyes, she was still in the little glade where they slept last night. Astoria sat by the fire watching her.

Soph.

My cell phone wakes me at seven. Once I remember where I am, I notice that Tess is doing push-ups by the foot of her bed. I don't care if she's a jock, but I hope this doesn't mean she has a body image problem. She shouldn't, since her body is very nice, but plenty of girls do. I want to ask her about it, but she's really working herself hard and I don't want to interrupt. After push-ups, she turns onto her back and does sit-ups.

I mumble, "Good morning," and go into the bathroom to shower.

We walk down to breakfast, and I work up the courage to ask Tess if she knows anything about admissions at Minerva College. She shakes her head. I think she must hate me for being flippant about military service last night. I can't think what to say about it. Maybe Gordon will text me back today. He's good at helping me pull my foot out of my mouth. I'm not wrong. The military *does* fight wars and kill people. How can that not be bad? I can't believe it's really a "great place for women." Hasn't Tess heard about all those sexual harassment problems? But Tess is certainly entitled to her opinion, not to mention her future.

A heavy snow comes down during breakfast, piling up on the sills outside the dining room's picture windows. It's beautiful. It almost never snows this much in New York, and when it does it quickly turns dirty until it disappears. After last night's rubber chicken, even the cardboard-y waffles taste good if I douse them from the bottle marked "Real Maple Syrup from New Hampshire," which we pass around. Joan soon tells us to finish up and clear our places so we can begin our first session.

Professor Forsythe announces that we are going to split into four groups, each led by a different adult: the Professor, Joan, Celestine, and Grace. Everyone will discuss what they write and where they want to go with it. Dialogue is encouraged—I guess the whole conference is about us being chosen for how our work is interconnected. We walk into a conference room with several large tables surrounded by chairs.

They put me in Professor Forsythe's group, just what I hoped. I'm with Orly, Chris, Tess, Clover, Janaye, and Yin. I bet this is what Minerva will be like, with Professor Forsythe choosing me to join her seminars. I look around at the other girls and wonder if any of them will end up at Minerva. Tess isn't interested, obviously, but I can see myself at college with some of the others. After her invitation-only poetry seminar, Professor Forsythe will edit my poem for a national journal. Then I'll go with Clover to the student union for a nitro brew or hang out in the dorm lounge with Janaye.

I sit next to Orly and smile at her, but she is not making eye contact. Clover sits next to me, and I'm fine with that. I don't want to sit next to Tess this morning. She sits on the other side of Professor Forsythe, and Chris sits down next to her. Figures. Tess pulls away, squirming when Chris whispers in her ear.

Once we're seated, Professor Forsythe smiles and looks around the table. "Good morning again. This session is a chance for you to tell us about your writing and what you want to do with it at this workshop, and to hear each other's reactions. I'll start. I'm Helen Forsythe. I am an academic, so my writing is analytical prose. But I am no stranger to creative writing. I concentrate on comparative literature. This semester, I am hard at work on a history of structure and rhyme scheme in Western poetry from the twelfth to the nineteenth centuries. I teach English composition, including poetry and fiction writing, at Minerva College, which will host us for an event later this week."

Wow. It sounds as if Professor Forsythe's current project lines up almost squarely with what I want to do here. I am about to say that, to introduce my work, when she cuts me off. "Tess, why don't you tell us about yourself and your writing?"

So Tess is first. Her eyes widen, and she darts a look toward Chris. "I'm Tess." Her voice wavers. "I'm from Castleton, New Hampshire. I write fan fiction online. Most of it is based on a television show called *The Witches' Circle*, which has two women as principal characters, Daphne and Astoria." She pauses, catches my eye across the table, and says in a shaky voice, "I know some people think fan fiction is lame, but in creating different storylines, I am trying to use magic as a symbol of a different kind of femininity, one which is based on women's skills, not their traditional roles." Chris stares at Tess. Tess seems to know that because, even while keeping her eyes focused on the table in front of her, she shrinks farther away. "Also, I don't always like what the show does with its plotlines. I change things to make the characters more powerful and less stereotyped. Umm…" Blushing, she ducks her head. "I guess for this workshop I want to write an ending to my current story that is pretty different from the season cliffhanger. I don't think I've figured out what that is yet, but I'm leaning toward having one of the witches find out she has a new extra-magical power which she doesn't quite understand how to use, and describing how she masters it."

Tess's speech makes me reconsider what I thought about her fan fiction. Maybe she doesn't just repeat dialogue from TV witches. She is writing about inherent female power, not about girls trying to become empowered or serve their country. I like that—there's so much feminist fiction out there that is about bringing women to the table and getting them into positions of authority, responsibility, and confidence. Tess is saying that they are already powerful, and how they understand and use their power is important. She's also writing about the women using that power for themselves instead of serving men or children.

But Chris offers a different opinion. Cocking her head, she turns toward Tess as if she cannot believe what she is hearing.

"I'm Chris. I'm from Dallas and, sorry, but fan fiction is pretty derivative. I think it's a cop-out. If you are going to use characters already out there, you should be writing nonfiction. And if you're going to write fiction, make it up yourself." She rolls her eyes and looks at Janaye, who is seated at the foot of the table. Janaye nods.

I expect Professor Forsythe to counterbalance Chris, but she goes along with it. "Tess, your *fan* fiction is very interesting, but your colleague, Chris, has a point. Why do you write fan fiction?"

Tess blanches. She actually goes pale. Her eyes were wide before, but now they're like saucers. Her mouth opens like a goldfish's, but nothing comes out. Professor Forsythe asks us, "Would anyone like to say anything else about Tess's work?"

I think this is unfair. Even though I thought the same thing last night and I barely know Tess, I don't like Chris's tone or that she's trying to make points with the rest of us by picking on Tess.

"I would," I say and am surprised by how worked up I am. "I think a little history and a little literature show that throwing shade at fan fiction is ridiculous. If you say it's 'derivative,' you might as well criticize the Romans for taking the Greek gods, renaming them, and changing their stories. Myths and legends grew as they were changed, embellished, and turned into longer works with different structures and outcomes."

I look at Chris when I say this. She glares back. I don't stop. This is what my mother calls "soapboxing." "I'm Soph, I'm from the City, and I write poetry. I want to be able to create structured poems like English and Italian sonnets. But getting back to fan fiction, do you think Shakespeare's characters aren't original?

Because I think Julius Caesar and Antony and Cleopatra were 'already out there,' not to mention four Henrys, two Richards and a John—"

Professor Forsythe interrupts. Her face bears a tight smile, and she says, "Sophie, maybe someone else would like to weigh in on *fan* fiction," again emphasizing "fan." Ouch. How can she not remember my name? I said it about twenty seconds ago *and* I cleared her plate last night. I'm trying too hard to impress her with how much I know and how well I fit in.

Yin, who's sitting next to Janaye with Chris, pipes up, "My name's Yin. I'm from Buffalo. I don't get why you say Shakespeare is *fan* fiction." Yin emphasizes "fan" the same way Professor Forsythe did.

Oh, lord, between the ganging up and the literary obliviousness, I might as well be at my mother's club on Park and 64th. This is the girl Professor Forsythe invited? "I'm saying *fan* fiction," I imitate Professor Forsythe's emphatic pronunciation, "is making fiction out of other characters. If you take a character from history or myth or another work and give that character a chance to grow and experience things that they didn't before, well, that's actually writing in a well-established tradition. I also think that if you criticize its validity, then you're rejecting a lot of literature that I bet you don't mean to reject. If I want to write sonnets like Shakespeare did, that shouldn't be a problem."

I look around the table. Tess stares down, frozen in place. Chris looks pissed, but some of the other girls are nodding at me. Professor Forsythe raises one eyebrow. Mimicking her was probably a mistake. Okay, definitely a mistake. My mother would kill me. Orly raises her hand, drawing Professor Forsythe's attention.

"I think Soph has a good point. I would add satire and musicals to her list. If writers were limited to wholly original characters, we'd lose all kinds of shows. *Rent* is based on *La Bohème*, which is an Italian opera based on a French book. So it is *derivative* too.

"I'm saying this because I am interested in how characters in stories change and also how they change across stories. So, I have done some research about how stories evolve and continue. I just started reading the original *Wizard of Oz*, to see how the story differs from the book *Wicked*, which uses the same characters but turns the Wicked Witch into someone sympathetic and likable."

Professor Forsythe smiles at Orly.

I can't keep my mouth shut. "And getting back to Shakespeare, *West Side Story* was based on *Romeo and Juliet*, which Shakespeare lifted from an earlier English poet, Arthur Brooks. Brooks didn't think it up either. The story was already a hundred years old and had been adapted twice in other languages. Is that *derivative*?" I emphasize the last word. I nod at Orly, who looks at me and then away. Out of the corner of my eye, I see Chris smirk, turn to Yin and Janaye, and whisper something. Yin nods but Janaye frowns. I catch Tess's eye. I hope she understands I'm sympathetic.

Tess begins to say something, but Professor Forsythe wants to move on. It's maddening. Maybe she's not even worth impressing.

"All right, great discussion. Chris, why don't you go next."

Chris is now wide-eyed; she deserves to feel nervous. But then she says, with confidence, "I plan to be a journalist. I'm particularly interested in covering women's issues and the relationships among groups of women in positions of relative power." When Chris says "women," she glares at Orly. Orly stares blankly back. What's *that* about?

I'm still so wound up that I can't keep my mouth shut. "Do you consider yourself to be a feminist, Chris?" I do. I believe in calling out misogyny and I am against those old binary definitions. Every woman has to be, given our obvious history of oppression.

Chris turns her glare to me. "I *am* a feminist and I hope we all are at this conference. Women have to stand together for their own safety and against anything that undermines it." Her eyes flick back to Orly. I can't tell what's going on between them. Maybe I should be grateful. Even though Tess and I have virtually nothing in common, at least she's polite, which is what I was supposed to be at this conference. I'd better shut up right now or I'm going to blow this whole thing.

Orly looks at Chris as if she's worried. Then she shifts in her seat and asks a question. "What about spirituality, though, and the broadened concept of femininity? Isn't that power in itself?" I'm starting to like Orly. She's smart.

Professor Forsythe breaks in. "Let's try to go light on politics. We want to focus on what type of writing you do and how you want to develop it. Chris, would you care to tell us where you want to go with your work?"

Chris responds, "I think you're asking the wrong question, frankly. As a journalist, my work is based on what goes on in the world. I want to go where the news is. I want to find it, expose it, analyze it, and relate it to women's power and safety."

Professor Forsythe nods, but withholds comment. I am surprised when Orly asks a pointed question. "Chris, do you write about women relative only to other women or are you more inclusive?"

Chris appears dumbfounded, then knits her brows as if the question angers her. "I don't know why you are asking me about women," she says pointedly. Out of the corner of my eye, I see Orly's jaw tighten. Professor Forsythe is about to say something when Chris says, "But I follow stories. Whatever comes up is what I have to react to." She sounds defensive, and still angry.

Professor Forsythe tries to open up the conversation again. "I wonder if anyone else might like to comment. This conversation is for the whole group, not only a few." I recognize that Chris hasn't answered the question, and I bet Orly does too. I'm through with my soapbox, though. I need to stop digging myself a bigger hole. Tess's eyes shift from Orly to Chris, then linger on Orly, but she doesn't say anything.

The "discussion" continues. Everyone else tries to be polite. Yin describes her blog, which is about language and identity. She uses elements of free verse but also short nonfiction pieces. I'm intrigued and ask for the link. Professor Forsythe doesn't seem to notice my attempt to make friends. Orly and Chris spend the rest of the session staring each other down. I feel as if I'm in the middle of a weird argument without knowing what the sides are or who started it. It's only the second day. Sometimes girls make me tired.

✳   ✳   ✳

During the break, Mom texts me.

[FROM MOTHER TO SOPH] *Darling, don't forget, presentation interviews in a month. See if anyone there has already had theirs.*

She ends it with a little crown emoji. She and Mrs. Peckett act as if everyone wants to walk through a ballroom in their white dress on the arm of some stupid guy. Puh-lease.

[FROM SOPH TO MOTHER] *Not that type of crowd, Mom.*

[FROM MOTHER TO SOPH] *Have you introduced yourself to Mrs. Forsythe?*

Predictable Mom, but not a question I need right now.

[FROM SOPH TO MOTHER] *Yes. Last night.*

I don't tell her it isn't going very well.

My mom responds with a smiling emoji. I'm tempted to send back the rolling eyes one.

Tess.

I HATE GOING FIRST IN those group things. I hate that I know exactly what I mean and exactly what I want to say in my head, but I'm never sure when it's okay to say it out loud. And when I go first I can't figure out the rules before I have to talk. But I'm surprised when Soph stands up for me. I wonder if she already knows what's going on between Chris and Orly. She's really passionate when she talks. It's hard not to watch her get all excited.

My mind wanders to the interview question I left in my knapsack. *Describe a recent incident where you took the lead.* Part of me thinks Soph is brave. And part of me thinks that in New York, people must be able to say whatever they want and no one ever gives them trouble. That's not what happens in Castleton. I guess it really is a different world.

We finally go around the whole room, and everyone else talks about their work. Nobody else gets criticized as harshly as I did—everyone is a little uncomfortable. Most people write fiction or poetry. Orly says she is working on a memoir about growing up in the South. She talks about her childhood as though it happened a long time ago, almost to a different person. Chris doesn't say anything to her, but everyone else nods.

Soph is working on a poem about trying to find love but not knowing where to find it. She wants to write English-style sonnets, but the rhyme scheme is too hard, so she's only done an Italian-style one so far. Not that the poem is written in Italian, but the rhyme scheme is different: couplets for Italian, something more complicated for English. She says she's attracted to the challenge of reducing emotion and experience into structured, rhythmic expressions and that she is drawn to the sonnet forms. It all sounds pretty complicated to me, and I wonder again if I'm in over my head. These girls were chosen from all over the country because they're such good writers. When no one comments, Professor Forsythe asks Soph what she hopes to accomplish this week. Soph gives her a big smile—weren't they just arguing about my fan fiction? She says she's having trouble going beyond couplets, and that she hopes Professor Forsythe will help her.

Chris flares her nostrils, but Yin seems intrigued. I don't quite get most of these girls. Soph is very serious when she talks about her writing; and the way she stood up for fan fiction was really nice. She isn't just a spoiled city kid—she's here to work hard on her writing, as I am. But she has no problem sticking up for people who aren't the same as she is and she really isn't shy about confronting opinions she disagrees with. I wish I knew how she learned that. I find myself paying close attention to Soph. She is clearly a leader. The other girls listen to her, and even Professor Forsythe was respectful when Soph stuck her neck out about fan fiction.

At the break, Soph makes a point of trying to talk to Professor Forsythe. She says she's interested in applying to Minerva College next fall. "You have one of the strongest writing programs in the country," she explains, "and I want to learn from you."

Professor Forsythe doesn't seem any more impressed with Soph than she did with me. "Why don't you focus on this week, Sophie," she says. I wince as she messes up Soph's name *again*. "There's plenty to learn before you apply to colleges." She turns away and asks Yin to help her distribute handouts for the second half of the session. I can tell Soph is upset even though she doesn't say anything else.

I go over to her and ask, "Is it that important to you to go to Minerva?"

She narrows her eyes at me. "Why, are you applying there too?"

"Me?" I laugh. "No, I'm a senior. Anyway, Minerva is much too fancy for me. My family wouldn't send me there." I don't say my family could never in a million years afford to send me there to waste four years writing stories. "I've been there for school field trips, and we used to drive up for their Winter Carnival every year. They always build these ice sculptures. There's a big bonfire in the middle of the quad. I think it was last weekend, but the sculptures might still be up when we visit later this week." One of the planned activities of the conference is a campus tour and a faculty reception at the Minerva College English department next weekend.

I pull up pictures of the sculptures on my phone to show Soph, and she's fascinated. She asks about the campus. I say, "I'm surprised you're interested in Minerva. It's pretty, but it's also pretty isolated."

"So what?" she says, as Professor Forsythe calls us all back to our seats. "Minerva is one of the oldest schools around. It has tons of traditions." That seems odd coming from her. The one thing I wouldn't call Soph is traditional.

Daddy always says that he learned to live with lots of different kinds of people in the military and that, despite their differences, they were all the same underneath; the guy from Alabama wanted to make it home safely the same way my dad did. That makes sense to me. I take a breath and hope that maybe Soph and I can be friends.

✳ ✳ ✳

From Soph Alcazar's Writing Journal,
February 11, 2018

Unfairness blossoms here at every turn.
I try to impress, but my stomach churns.

Chapter Six

From the Fan Fiction Unbound Archive,
posted by con Tessaofthecastle:

By the fire that night, they shared the last of the dried meat Astoria had in her pack. They would have to hunt or forage for nuts or berries in the morning. Daphne's head hurt. She sighed and, leaning against a tree, tried to find a more comfortable position. She closed her eyes, listening to the crackle of the fire and the rustle of small creatures in the forest nearby. As she tried to concentrate, she felt the pain in her head lift slowly, like a scarf being pulled from her throat by gentle hands. When she opened her eyes, Astoria was watching her in the dark.

"Is your head better?" Astoria asked.

Soph.

AT THE END OF LUNCH, Professor Forsythe announces that she, Joan, Celestine, and Grace have determined the assignments for our group projects. "An important part of your development as writers is to train you to write in new ways. That means interacting and working with people whose own work is different from yours, but contains or does something which can bring your work to a whole new level. This is why we asked you to describe your work and discuss it with each other this morning.

"You may find conflict at first in your group, but how you bridge the gaps between and among your partners is the very essence of writing for a broader range of readers than merely those who share your interests. This afternoon, you'll meet and brainstorm about how you can collaborate on a written project which combines what each of you does into a single piece. The four of us will circulate among the groups to facilitate your discussion, but you will collectively control your own work product. We'll spend the remainder of the afternoon in the conference room, but this time divided into the separate, smaller groups. Then we'll come back together for the evening meal."

I get put in a group with Gabriela, Yin, whom I haven't figured out, and a girl named Ellen, who writes songs. Everyone is excited. Yin was the only one I was worried about, but she's into how words sound near and next to each other, which works well with the rest of us.

Gabriela's poetry is less structured than mine. She shows us some of it, and I like the way it's moody but then uplifting. She writes about loss and how you can still love someone when you lose them, like her dad who died when she was young or the best friend who moved away.

I can't help wondering if her friend was actually her girlfriend, so I ask, "What happened to your friend?"

Gabriela frowns. "Oh, he went off to college. We skype a lot, but he was like a brother and it's not the same as having him around." Her face brightens. "A guy at my new high school asked me out—if it weren't so far, I'd introduce them so I could see what Max thinks of Evan."

So, not her girlfriend, and she's straight or bi. I wasn't interested in her or anything, but it would be nice if there was another gay girl or two here. At the midafternoon break, Ellen and Yin talk about their boyfriends and ask Gabriela about hers. I don't say much, but I think maybe this is what Lally feels like when Gordon and I are talking about our crushes or Mibs is off with Greg. I'll text the three of them about it later and see what they think.

After we come back together, Yin asks us all, "How do we take the stuff we write and do a single piece? The rest of you all work in verse, but my thing is my blog with some free verse."

Ellen comes up with the best suggestion. "What if we do a variation on a ballad? There's room in that for everyone. As long as we develop a storyline and some distinct forms that we repeat in short stanzas, everyone can participate in her own format, including blog posts. Would that work for you, Yin?"

"I guess. The format would be fine. I want to think, though, about whether I do fictional blog posts or not. How do we figure out a subject or a story?"

This is where we get stuck.

Grace joins us and suggests, "Why don't you sleep on it? Time's almost up. Sometimes the hardest part is figuring out what form you are going to write in, and you've done that very well. When I was here a few years ago, everyone was like them." She gestures to the group with Tess in it. Joan is sitting with them talking, but no one is nodding. Chris's arms cross tightly over her chest, and Peggy scowls. Tess stares down, as if she wishes she could be somewhere else.

Grace sees our reaction and laughs. "Oh, they'll work it out. We did. By the time everyone builds snowsisters, everything will be fine."

Tess.

CHRIS AND I ARE TEAMED with two other girls, Peggy and Keisha. After what Chris said last night at the Mocktail Party, I'm pretty unhappy to find that she and I are in the same group. But the cat is about out of the bag at this point. I mean, she knows from this morning's introduction that I'm the one at the conference who writes fan fiction, and I know exactly what she thinks of that. What I have to figure out now is how to convince her to work with me.

I guess this is one of those uncomfortable things I'm going to have to get used to, especially after I graduate, so I pick up my notebook and go to the corner of the room where she sits, thinking that we can talk. All the other girls are breaking into small groups.

My dad used to tell Molly and me stories about the first Iraq war and how he was deployed with a guy named Richard Oliver. Apparently, he was such a jerk that most of the guys called him "Dick All-Over." He talked all the time and constantly insulted the guys in the squad, which my dad said got really old when you were all living packed in a barracks, far from your family. He used to moo when my dad walked by. My dad is a third-generation dairy farmer and he's extremely proud of our farm. We supply milk to all the New England states. My dad works hard every day. Having someone he didn't even know make fun of his home and his business was tough on him.

But Dick was a talented tank driver, even if he didn't know when to stop talking trash, and one day he drove my dad's convoy through crossfire and never so much as blinked. He saved ten guys' lives. My dad said that taught the whole squad that everyone has their strengths and you need to keep looking for them, even if you don't like someone.

So, okay, I need to find out Chris's strengths. I can hear Daddy's voice saying, "You know not to walk away from a job before it's done…"

I sit down and, before Chris can say anything, I go first, because I'm not going to let her steamroll me again, like this morning during the talk with Professor Forsythe. "So, Chris does journalism, and the rest of us write fiction. Anybody have any ideas for how to put something together that combines everybody's interests?"

Nobody says anything and I'm confused about what to say next. I don't know how to do this. Across the room, Soph is already laughing at an idea of Gabriela's. God, I am really bad at this. What makes me think I'm going to be able to be a leader?

But then Keisha suggests that we do fiction that takes place a long time ago and involves a fictional character that we all know, so we can work in the fan fiction genre. Peggy chimes in that it could be Maizy Donovan, that journalist in the old Ultraman comic strip, so we can work in both journalism and fan fiction by giving her a personal life and a storyline of her own outside of the adventures of Ultraman. I take notes and I think the idea is sounding kind of cool, better than anything I could have come up with.

Chris sits back and says flatly, "That isn't going to work."

That stops all of us in our tracks. I ask her why.

She says, "Because the whole thing is fiction. You guys can write that, but I write real stories about true events that actually happen. You would need to come up with something that includes investigative journalism." I notice she doesn't say that "she" or even "we" would have to come up with it.

I take a breath and try to tell her that the journalism part comes from what Maizy is working on, but she won't agree. Even when Keisha and Peggy attempt to convince her to try it, she just shakes her head. I'm wondering how she thinks we can investigate something from here in only a week.

"Well," I say, taking a different approach. "What do you suggest we do, Chris?"

She shrugs and says, "I don't care what you guys write. I'm here to improve my own writing and expand my resumé for college applications. I'm going to figure out how Orly got in, since he's really a guy. I want to know if he lied on his application and if Professor Forsythe knows and didn't tell the rest of us and why. This is a safety issue for women. I think that sounds like a pretty good story. Y'all can do what you want."

The session breaks up, so we can go down for the afternoon break. Keisha, Peggy, and I aren't sure how we can persuade Chris to work with us, and I'm definitely not going anywhere near the thing with Orly. First of all, that's none of my business. Second, I'm not here to make trouble for anyone. But it seems... wrong. Orly's group in the corner is talking about something that I can't hear, and Orly has this little smile on her face as though she's having a nice time. She isn't bothering anyone and, from what I can tell, she's working with her group way better than Chris is working with ours. I see Soph again. She laughs at something one of the other girls says. From across the room, I can tell it's Soph laughing. She's waving her hands around, explaining something to her group as though she's really excited about her project. I wish I could pick up my stuff and just tiptoe across the room and sit down next to her.

I text Joey quickly, to tell him I don't know how to make Chris work with us, and he texts back.

[FROM JOEY TO TESS] *What's her problem?*

I don't have time to text him again, so I shove my phone back in my pocket and go to break.

Soph is there, but she's already surrounded by people as we help ourselves to cookies and coffee or tea in the lounge with the big fireplace. Janaye shows Soph something on her phone, and even Orly is kind of stuck to her right shoulder. I stand next to Keisha and ask her about where she lives in Washington, DC. Her mom works for NASA, and her dad teaches at a university there. She tells me she's a fan of *The Witches' Circle*, and suddenly I can breathe again. I tell her about my story, and it turns out she knows it. Before you know it, we're talking about the show and the fandom and the different stories she reads. For the first time since I got here, I think I might belong. Keisha takes me as seriously as Soph did this morning and she loves my latest story; she keeps telling me how cool it is to meet the author. No one has ever called me an author.

When we go back into our groups, I think about what Joey texted and I try again with Chris.

"Is there a problem with Orly? I mean, has she done something that makes you uncomfortable?"

Chris frowns and shakes her head.

"You don't get it. He's not a girl. I found out by accident because we're roommates."

"Yeah," says Keisha, "but did he—I mean did *she* do something to hurt you? She's been totally nice to me. She lent me some Chapstick last night in the van."

Chris turns her attention to Keisha and rolls her eyes. "God, could you people be more naive?" She looks at both of us. Peggy sits silently. "This is an awesome story. This is supposed to be a conference to empower young women writers. So, first of all, it should be women. And second of all, what would y'all's parents think about *you* rooming with a guy you don't even know?"

She has a point. If what Chris says is true, my dad would be furious if he knew I was rooming with Orly. But, even so, I don't think that's what Chris is focused on. I think she wants an article published somewhere. That's what's making me uncomfortable. I try to make her focus on the writing we're supposed to be doing.

"I think I get that you want to do some real journalism for this conference and we're all fiction writers, but this is supposed to be a group project. Do you have any ideas for what we could do that could solve everyone's problem and still have us work together?"

She blinks at me and says, in that flat drawling voice, "Do your own project. I'll do mine. No one tells. Everyone's happy at the end. You put your names on your group project, and I send my work to feminist blogs and online magazines to expose how a supposed 'women's writing conference' actually includes guys who put young women's safety in jeopardy." Without saying another word, she gets up and leaves the room.

So much for working as a group. I'm clearly not able to lead Chris anywhere. I'm confused by her attitude, though. She isn't saying she wants to switch rooms or tell Professor Forsythe about Orly. In fact, she wants us to keep her secret while she does her investigation. None of that sounds right to me. My dad might not want me rooming with Orly, but he sure as heck wouldn't be happy with me doing it and spying on her behind her back at the same time. His voice comes back to me: "Make us proud, Tess." I came to this workshop to learn how to write and to try to figure out how to answer that darn question about leadership. None of this mess is going to help me figure that out. Besides, I'm barely starting to make friends with my own roommate. Maybe I should focus on that for now.

⁎　⁎　⁎

From Soph Alcazar's Writing Journal,
February 11, 2018

It's good to be with fellow balladeers.
But she, I sense, is not with musketeers.

Chapter Seven

From the Fan Fiction Unbound Archive,
posted by conTessaofthecastle:

The next morning dawned cool and cloudy. Astoria was quiet as they packed the remainder of their food and covered the campfire. Daphne tried to coax her into speaking while they walked away from camp, pointing out a red cardinal perched on a branch overhead. But Astoria shook her head silently.

"I don't know what to tell you," Daphne finally said, picking her way over a fallen branch. "Perhaps you shouldn't have come with me."

Astoria replied sharply, "Perhaps you shouldn't doubt me."

Soph.

BACK IN OUR ROOM, TESS is intent on tapping out a text. While she does that, I google "discrimination in the armed forces" and find some articles. There are alarming statistics about how many women get assaulted. I knew there were problems, but I never really paid attention to it before now. I'm not going to say anything to Tess though, at least not yet.

When she finishes texting, I pick up the thread of our earlier conversation. "I'm sorry, Tess, about disrespecting the military.

I had no idea... Well, I don't know anyone who's doing that." I don't know what else to say.

She sits up against the headboard of her bed and crosses her legs. She's wearing purple fleece socks tonight. "It's fine." She looks a little confused and asks, "Do you really not know anyone who's served in the military? Not your dad or your grandfather or an uncle?"

I explain that I don't.

"Don't you have any family traditions like with the king or something?"

"Well, yes, sort of. Not military, though. I'm supposed to make my debut next winter. Both of my parents expect me to do that, but I'm not going to."

"What does that mean, 'make your debut'? It sounds like something in a movie."

"It means being presented as a debutante, at a ball, in a white gown, all made up with the hair and nails. I'm not doing it. My mother doesn't understand why I hate the idea."

"Wow!" She seems impressed. "A real ball, like the Disney movies? Did your mom do it?"

"Oh yes, of course. She did, and so did her mother and every woman on my father's side. I don't think it's like your family's tradition, Tess. We're not serving a country or anything."

"What's so bad about it? When I was a kid I used to watch those movies and I always wanted to go to a ball with all the gowns and tiaras and chandeliers. It looked magical." The dreamy expression on her face irritates me.

"It totally objectifies women! It's like being presented as the prize pig of the county fair! And the crowd there, lily-white, über-rich, all social register. It's totally elitist, very white privilege." That snaps her out of her daydream. Her eyes focus on me. She picks up her water bottle and takes a sip, as if she's trying to figure something out.

"I don't think it sounds so terrible, Soph. You said earlier that you liked traditions. Your parents must think it's important. Is it that different from taking your first communion?"

I don't know how to explain this to her. If I told her about how it was something my family's been doing for hundreds of years, let alone that people with titles will be there, she'd think I was crazy not to go. "Well, making your debut is not religious. And you have to be proposed and approved by a committee."

"Hmm." She giggles, a funny noise that at first makes me wonder if she's making fun of me. But she's not. "That sounds familiar to me."

"Why?"

"Well, I'll probably end up enlisting in the army when I finish high school, but I'm applying to West Point first. If I get in there, they'll give me a free education, and then I'll serve. They would even let me major in English, so I could become a better writer. But first I have to impress the admissions committee. My interview is in two weeks, and I'm pretty nervous."

"West Point is the one near the City, right? It must be hard to get in."

"Yes. The application process is long and pretty complicated. A candidate has to prove a whole bunch of things, like athletic ability and leadership. Plus, you have to be nominated by someone in the government. You need nominations from a congressman or a senator. Or," she gives me a sad smile, "the vice president or president, if you're lucky. Less than ten percent of the applicants become cadets. I'm really worried about the interview. My grades are pretty good, and I have some of the things they want for extracurriculars, but they ask all kinds of questions that I don't have good answers to… I probably won't get in." She shrugs as if she doesn't care, but her face is flushed and she hugs her chest to her knees.

Tess doesn't look at all like my idea of a military cadet, but this gives me an idea. "Hey, maybe I could help, Tess. My friend Mibs, her uncle is the vice president. I could text her now, and I bet she would ask him to do it—"

Tess's face stops me. Is she mad? I'm trying to be nice.

"You know the vice president?" she asks.

"Well, no, not personally," I say, "but my friend Mibs does, and I'm sure I could get her to ask him to write you a letter."

"Soph, I barely know you, let alone your friend or the vice president. Thanks, but I wrote to my congressman and our senators. If one of them comes through for me, that will be the best I can do."

The expression on her face is skeptical, so I try again.

"Tess, I swear, the vice president is her uncle. He's her mother's brother. He got them into the White House to meet the president. If the vice president's recommendation would help you get into West Point, why shouldn't I ask her to call him for you? I can text her right now." I pick up my phone and wait.

She looks at me like I'm an idiot, and I fume. But then she sighs and straightens her legs, flexes her feet, and points her toes. I'm not sure why, but I can't stop watching her purple feet, flexing and pointing.

"Soph, it's the military. If they let me into West Point and I actually manage to graduate, I'll have a commission in the Army as a second lieutenant."

I start to say I get it, but she interrupts me. Her expression is intense.

"That question I have to answer? For the admissions panel in a couple of weeks? That question is about leadership." She leans over the side of the bed and rifles through her knapsack until she finds a crumpled piece of paper, which she reads. "Describe a recent incident where you took the lead." She peers over the paper as if she just explained something very important. I don't know what it is. She sighs, props her back against her headboard, pulls her knees up under her chin, and hugs them.

"If a war broke out, Soph, I would need to be a leader of my troops. They would depend on me to make the right calls. And if I didn't make the right calls, those troops would obey me anyway. I have to know what I'm doing, and the Army has to know that I'm the right candidate for that kind of responsibility. The reason it's so hard to get into West Point is because they are making sure they pick the right people to lead. It's not about knowing the right politician. It's not about being able to fake who you are. It means something to hold a command. If the wrong person holds it, soldiers die."

Tess.

EVEN THOUGH BOTH SOPH AND I seem to be trying, we don't seem any closer to figuring each other out. I'm not sure why that's bothering me so much, but it is. I still haven't mentioned Chris to her. I go down to dinner a little early, leaving Soph texting someone on her phone. I want to ask one of the instructors if there is a computer I can use this week. Orly is in the lounge reading a book, and I'm about to go say hi when Chris comes up behind her and asks her questions, which seems weird, because they room together. I don't understand why Orly is reading down here or why Chris followed her.

Chris asks, "What was it like growing up outside Atlanta, Orly?"

Without knowing why, I step back into the hall so they can't see me. I should not be eavesdropping, I know that. But I can't seem to turn away.

Orly is noncommittal. "Probably a lot like it was growing up in Dallas, Chris." She's clearly uncomfortable.

Chris is not letting up. "Are you from a suburb or a small town?"

Orly fidgets in her chair, but she answers, "A small town."

Then I figure out exactly what Chris is doing. She's conducting an interview, for her secret investigation. But Orly doesn't know what's going on. I'm about to go back in and interrupt when Professor Forsythe sweeps in from the hallway behind me and calls out to Orly. I cringe, hoping Professor Forsythe doesn't realize what I was doing. I make a mental note to try to avoid Professor Forsythe.

"Chris, excuse us, I need to steal Orly away for a bit. We're working on a revision before supper."

Orly grabs her laptop and closes her book. She and Professor Forsythe walk down the hall to one of the empty conference rooms.

Chris eyes me sharply as I come tentatively into the lounge. "What was that?" she asks me. "Now they're giving him private writing instruction?"

I want to tell her to stop this, now. Instead I shrug and turn away without answering.

The other girls file in for dinner. I turn to say hi to Gabriela and Yin, as Soph comes down the stairs with Clover. She's practically bouncing on her feet as they laugh together. Janaye taps her shoulder at the bottom of the stairs to share something on her phone.

A few minutes later they open the dining room, and Professor Forsythe and Orly come back down the hallway talking to each other. Chris types something into her phone before sitting down.

I miss Joey.

❋ ❋ ❋

From Soph Alcazar's Writing Journal,
February 11, 2018

Again, I try to get where she comes from.
But when I can help, she tells me I'm dumb.

Chapter Eight

After walking quietly for a couple of hours, Astoria stopped to adjust her shoe. While Daphne waited for her, Astoria said, "Daphne, you have to stop believing you forced me to leave the Coven. If you don't understand why I needed to come with you and take this risk, you won't ever believe that we will succeed."

Daphne thought about protesting, about explaining why she felt responsible, but Astoria's fierce expression made her stop.

"All right," Daphne said after a pause, "but I need you to be honest with me. If you ever want to turn back, you must let me know."

"Trust me to speak my own mind." Astoria moved past her on the narrow path.

Soph.

WE HAVE FREE TIME AFTER dinner. Professor Forsythe suggested we use it for "independent study and socializing," so I go to the lounge and sit on a couch. I'll try to find out more about Yin and how she got to know "Helen" Forsythe. Janaye sits next to me with her laptop.

"Seriously, that dinner?"

I know what she means. Chris and Orly served us chili tonight, but it wasn't very good. I don't know where they ordered it, but the delivery menu should be burned. "Yeah, not like El Original, right?"

"Don't know it, Soph. Is that one of your Uppah East Side things?"

"No," I protest, even though I know she's kidding. "It's Tenth and Forty-Eighth! They have awesome nachos, too."

Gabriela walks in. She must have overheard us. "They tried. Maybe the ingredients were bad—or the recipe."

Janaye shrugs.

I smile and try to pretend I knew they cooked it themselves. "I ate the cornbread. It was so sweet it was like a cupcake!"

Yin sits down on the other side of the lounge. While I try to figure out how to draw her into our conversation, Gabriela saves me by calling to her, "What's up, Yin? We're rudely complaining about dinner."

Yin makes a face. "I'm still hungry."

"Does anyone feel like going out?" I ask.

"You mean out to walk in the snow?" I guess there aren't many restaurants where Gabriela lives in Connecticut.

"No, I was thinking just go out somewhere and get something to eat. You know, there must be someplace."

Janaye is in. "Sounds cool to me. I've been sitting all day."

"No thanks. I'm beat. I don't think there's any place to go anyway." Gabriela's out.

I try Yin. "Do you want to join us?"

"Where is there around here?"

"I don't know. I can ask my roommate. She's from around here. Let's go!"

We leave Gabriela and traipse up the stairs. Tess looks up when we walk in. "Tess, we want to go out. Do you know any place around here?"

"Joey and I drove past a pizza place on the way in. It wasn't far. But I don't think we're supposed to leave the lodge without talking to Professor Forsythe."

Janaye isn't having any of that. "We won't tell them. If we go around the lounge to the front door, no one will notice."

"Pizza sounds really good right now," Yin says.

Tess looks around at all of us.

I'm impatient. "Tess, c'mon. We need you to show us where it is."

She hesitates, then gets up. "Oh all, right. They never actually said we couldn't go out."

"Should we invite anyone else?"

"How about Orly?" I don't wait for an answer. I stride across the hall and knock on Orly's door. She laughs when I tell her the plan.

"I know that dinner wasn't great, but you want me to go out? In this cold? No, thank you!"

"Orly, it will be fun. A bunch of us are going. You can borrow one of my scarves." She glances at the group coming out of our room and relents with a nod. We agree to meet at the front door.

On our way down the stairs, Tess and I run into Chris, who asks, "Where is everyone going?"

Tess invites her, and Chris thinks about it, but, as Orly comes down the stairs behind us, Chris shakes her head and goes up the stairs. It's a big relief to me. I wouldn't have asked her.

We meet at the front door; we've successfully evaded the adults, even Grace. Janaye has a cool, dark brown shearling coat on. Yin appears ready for the Arctic in a quilted thing with a huge hood, gloves, and a knit hat. Orly has on the same coat she wore yesterday, with a matching scarf and earmuffs. Tess is in pink, no surprise.

I pull the door open slowly so it doesn't make any sound. The cold air hits my face, making me wince. We sneak down the steps and stand in the driveway beyond the light from the lodge. "Okay, Tess, where to?"

"Down the driveway and to the left. I think it's about a mile."

Away from the lights of the lodge, it's pitch black. Huge pine trees tower over us on both sides of the plowed access road. It's a little spooky, frankly. The City is never this dark.

"A mile," Orly gasps. "In this cold? Y'all must have thought we made some *baaad* chili!"

I hope they're not having second thoughts. I assume Tess knows what she's doing. "C'mon, that's only twenty blocks. Janaye has to walk that far to get a subway in Brooklyn."

Janaye laughs. "Manhattanites, folks."

Nobody says anything. I forget that most people don't know how New York works or that Brooklyn and Manhattan are really different. Everyone here seems to think Janaye and I are from the same place. I suppose Janaye and I have more in common than we do with anyone else.

Tess finally says, "If we walk quickly, you won't feel the cold so much."

Orly sinks into her coat and follows Tess down the driveway.

Yin catches me shivering. "You people would never survive in Buffalo," she snorts.

"Is Buffalo colder than this?" Orly asks.

"Def," Yin responds. "The wind is always howling off Lake Erie. We get eight feet of snow every winter, and it's blinding. This is like a spring thaw."

Orly makes a clucking sound and pats one of her earmuffs.

"Keep your minds on the pizza—that should help," I add.

It does help. We walk down the driveway and make the left Tess mentioned. The road has streetlights but no sidewalk. At least it's plowed, so we aren't trudging through snow. We fan out across the road in a rough line. There's no traffic, and the stars are brighter than I've ever seen. Scattered here and there along the road are a few houses, most with smoke coming from chimneys and trucks in the driveways. After about ten minutes, we see the lights of town.

Tess points out our destination. "There: Granite State Pizza."

Sure enough, there's a little square building with a neon sign shaped like New Hampshire.

It's very small: two plastic booths in front and a counter with a cash register on the left. The doorbell rings as we come in and a man looks up from the cash register. He's wearing a white T-shirt, even though it's freezing out; he's built like he knows how to eat a pizza as well as make one. He doesn't say anything.

Orly moans with pleasure, "Oh, that heat feels wonderful." She's right. The place is really warm. It smells like oregano and marinara sauce.

Janaye walks up to the counter and says to the man, "Can you make me a Bee Sting? Small?"

The man stares at Janaye, obviously confused. "A what?" he asks.

"A Bee Sting pizza. Oh, and do you make juice here?"

"Juices? Yeah, there's apple juice and cranberry juice in the cooler."

Tess taps Janaye on the shoulder. Either she's blushing or her cheeks are pink from the cold. "Um, I don't think they have any of that on the menu, Janaye."

"But they're so good. Right, Soph? You've been to Roberta's."

"What's a Bee Sting?" Orly asks.

"They have spicy sausage with honey drizzled on them over the tomato sauce and cheese," I explain. "Yeah, Janaye, but I don't see them either." I point to a whiteboard above the counter with black plastic letters. It reads "large" and "small" and has a list of toppings. No honey. "No juicing, either."

"Oh, okay. Sorry."

Tess smiles at the guy behind the counter. "Granite State makes good pizza. We have one in Castleton." He smiles back at her, and I can tell it's going to be all right. She's not as mousy as I'd thought from our after-hours conversations. Maybe that's the military thing. "Let's just share a large. What does everyone like on top?"

We're all over the map on that one. No one wants to pick. Yin and Orly do that thing where they say they don't care and they'll have whatever. Janaye just seems confused by the lack of New York ingredients. Tess looks at me as if she's curious to see whether I'm going to be all weird like Janaye or adapt to my surroundings. She looks more comfortable here than she does back at the lodge, as if she's back in her own world. I'm for mushroom, but I don't want to be pushy. Tess looks around at everyone and suggests half sausage and half plain, since Janaye wanted sausage originally. We all shrug, so that's what we order. We each pay for a drink and look in the refrigerator case.

Janaye's not there yet. She looks at the bottles and says, "I guess no Boylan's, huh?"

"Janaye, we're *not* in Brooklyn anymore." I laugh. "Think of this as normcore eating."

"What's normcore?" With her accent, Orly makes it sound like "know'm cooor."

"It's hipster for Gap from twenty years ago—mom jeans and gray pullovers with little vees at the neck." Janaye rolls her eyes as she explains. Tess flashes us a hurt-feelings look. Oops.

Yin snorts. "You guys, there's a world out here beyond Brooklyn and Manhattan!" Tess nods and works up a small smile. She's cute when she smiles like that. She still has her pom-pom hat on her head. I should be nicer. Also, I remind myself to focus on Yin.

We pile into a booth. We don't really fit, but it's fun. We're all laughing as we take off our coats and Orly passes around napkins.

"So, do you blog about the Buffalo winters, Yin?" Professor Forsythe can't be that interested in the weather.

"No. I blog about what it's like to be a teenage girl in the twenty-teens. You know, popular culture, social pressure, and how our parents screwed up the world for us. Also, sometimes I write about what it's like to be an immigrant's kid."

"Wow. Interesting." And impressive, too. She might be stiffer competition than I guessed. "What's it called?" I might learn something from reading it.

"Yin Without Yang."

Janaye laughs. "What's the yin if a girl can't get some yang?"

"Since yin symbolizes the feminine, I intentionally cut out the masculine symbol of yang so I can put a good spin on it in my college essay. It doesn't mean I don't want a little yang myself, Janaye."

"Got it." We all laugh. Tess looks as if she doesn't get the joke.

"Oh, yang is so not my thing," I say.

Janaye jokes, "You mean 'thang,' right?"

Yin and I laugh, but Tess and Orly don't. Maybe I overstepped? I'm just putting it out there.

Tess.

WHEN THE PIZZA ARRIVES, EVERYONE goes for the plain half, even Janaye, who wanted sausage. Orly is watching her weight, and Yin is "mostly vegetarian." I wish they had said something before we ordered. We could have had mushroom like Soph wanted, which is my favorite too. I take a slice of the sausage. Granite State uses spicy Italian sausage, and that's pretty good back home. It turns out this is exactly the same. I feel better, even though most of what Soph and Janaye and Yin talk about doesn't make much sense.

Yin talks more about her blog and describes her complicated college admissions strategy. She's going to apply to twenty schools. She has visited nine of them so far. She plans to take the admissions tour when we visit Minerva later this week. Soph pays close attention to what Yin says. I tell them a little about the Oktoberfest that Minerva does every year and how they have a spring concert that Joey and I came for last April. We had to listen from behind the stage because we didn't have IDs, but the band was Maple Left from Montreal, one of Joey's favorites. We both sang along like idiots. After the concert, we walked around town and went for ice cream. Soph seems to like that story, so I'm glad I told her.

I'm sitting next to Orly. "Are you warmed up?"

She laughs. "Yes, for now. But I dread the walk back. I don't know how y'all do it in this cold."

"I liked hearing about your writing. What else are you doing?"

"Well, you know how you remember some things from when you were really little, but they seem different from what you remember from last week?"

I do.

"It's mostly that. When I was really young, we lived out in the country, near the South Carolina border. I remember things like the time my puppy got lost and we drove around all afternoon in Daddy's truck, looking for him. We moved to a town near Atlanta when I started fifth grade. Everything before then feels like it happened ages ago…"

Even though it's strange for a teenager to be writing a memoir, I know what she means. There's lots of things that I remember from being little, like going with MeMe and Gramps to the grocery store every Saturday and picking out a box of those little animal crackers or helping Daddy prepare taps for collecting sap during sugaring season. It was only a few years ago, but the details are hazy. I think it's nice that Orly keeps track of stories like that. I bet MeMe would like it if I write out some of my memories and give them to her before I leave next summer. It's hard to know how long it will be before I'm allowed to go home.

Being in the pizza place relaxes me. I have a moment of panic when the guy brings the check because I only brought twenty dollars with me this week and I have used almost half of it for my share and my drink, once Janaye figures out a tip. I hope there aren't going to be any more expenses like this. But I have to admit, once Soph and Janaye stop comparing everything to New York and I have food in my stomach, the evening is looking more like a success.

Yin and Soph talk about a summer camp in the Catskills they both went to as kids. Janaye asks Orly about her earrings.

Soph tells a funny story about trying to ask a girl out on a date in a coffee shop in New York and getting interrupted by the girl's boyfriend. "Hey," she shrugs, as though it was no big deal. "She was cute. I didn't know he was in the men's room. We had a moment."

She and Janaye and Yin all laugh. I have no idea where to look. No one at home would ever tell this story, and they certainly wouldn't laugh about it. But it feels good, watching other girls I don't know tell stories and make each other laugh and try to get along. Joey will like it when I tell him.

I ask Orly about her session with Professor Forsythe. "Did she ask all sorts of hard questions?"

"No. We read some of it and she pointed out how the words sounded together. I thought only about what they meant, but she suggested I choose words that sound like the feelings I want to convey. She's very smart, Professor Forsythe. That's why I asked to talk to her."

That catches Soph's attention.

"You mean she gave you a private critique?"

Orly nods.

"Did you set it up before you came? Is there a sign-up sheet somewhere?"

It's odd how intense Soph is about this subject. Orly seems taken aback, but she tells Soph what she knows. "No. She said anyone could ask. She told me that all the teachers are available. I thought I might ask Grace to look at my next chapter."

Soph frowns at me. "Why bother with Grace? Helen Forsythe is the important person to know here." She turns to Yin, "Right?"

"I guess." Yin shrugs. "I mean, she invited me to apply, but I don't really know her. And I think that getting into the conference and maybe doing some good work here is probably what colleges are looking for most. It's less important to have good recommendations than it is to have an impressive body of work."

These girls are really serious. At my school, most kids who are going to college are going to the state university in Durham. Nobody is that worried about anything other than how to pay for it.

I don't need college help and I want to stay as far away from Professor Forsythe as possible. I mention that I want help with integrating spells into my writing, when I realize that both Yin and Soph are poets.

Soph hesitates. She exchanges a look with Janaye before turning back to me. "Sure," she says. "I'd be happy to help. I don't really know anything about the show. But I could put together some couplets if that would work."

I'm happy that she agreed to help when I asked and nervous about showing her what I'm working on.

Soph asks Orly about Chris, and the mood changes. I tense up. Orly looks long and hard at Soph.

"I mean," Soph rolls her eyes, "Is she any friendlier behind closed doors? Or does she spend all night lecturing you about the proper literature to read and the appropriate response to every occasion?"

Orly is still staring at Soph. "It's fine," she says. "I'm fine."

Soph seems about to say something else when Yin jumps in, "Oh, Chris is really smart. She's just intense."

Then Orly adds, "Intense, yes. Making that chili surely was intense. We both read the recipe and added things, but she would barely talk to me. I think we both put in the chili powder. That might be why it came out so poorly."

Soph rolls her eyes. "I can only imagine she's already done a thorough investigation into how to make chili and found there is only her way!" Everyone laughs.

I pretend to yawn so that I can break up this conversation. "Better head back," I say. I have fifty push-ups to do before bed.

Everyone is still laughing as we go back into the cold, but I hear Soph talking low with Orly on the walk. I don't want to know what they're saying.

❋ ❋ ❋

From Soph Alcazar's Writing Journal,
February 11, 2018

Disappointed by chili, we venture out.
I try to determine my rival's clout.

Chapter Nine

*From the Fan Fiction Unbound Archive,
posted by conTessaofthecastle:*

*Clouds darkened the sky above the tree canopy as they
picked their way through the forest. Daphne stopped once or
twice to close her eyes and repeat the pathfinder chant. They
couldn't use the sun to guide them in this part of the woods,
and she wasn't at all sure that they were headed in the right
direction. She didn't say anything to Astoria, instead relying
on the chant. She'd know soon enough if it was wrong.*

Soph.

AFTER BREAKFAST ON MONDAY MORNING, we go into a large
conference room with Celestine. On one end is a big screen, and
Celestine tells us to make sure we can all see it.

"This morning, we are going to do an exercise called 'Show
and Tell.' It will seem more familiar to those of you who write
nonfiction, but it is useful for every writer. The first part is simple.
I want you to watch this short video." She dims the lights and the
screen brightens. She's right. It is short. When it ends, Celestine
turns off the monitor and puts the lights back on. She walks
around the long conference table handing each of us a blue exam
book and a pen, saying, "Now I want you each to write down

what you saw in the video, so that someone who reads what you're writing will know what happened."

I write: *In a school library, there are a few wooden tables and a girl sitting at one of the tables studying. She finishes what she's doing then stands up and leaves. A heavyset girl with short hair walks up to one of the tables, looking for the first girl, who was supposed to meet her there. Then she reaches under the table and picks up a messenger bag. She searches for the other girl again, but doesn't see her, so she shrugs and leaves.*

After we finish writing, Professor Forsythe, Joan, and Grace come into the room. Celestine says, "We're going to divide into four groups now. Each of us will take one of the four groups into another room. We'll read out names of our respective participants and you should follow us out. Bring what you've written and your pen."

Professor Forsythe calls my name and puts me in a group with Ellen, Peggy, Keisha, Yin, and Tess. We follow Professor Forsythe into a smaller room with a round table and a video screen. I sit between Ellen and Yin. My mother would be thrilled. I can hear her reminding me that I need to seize "every chance to make an excellent impression, darling." Get out of my head, Mom! But I *should* try to make up for that fan fiction fight I started yesterday. When we're seated, Professor Forsythe asks us to go around the room reading aloud what we wrote.

Ellen, the songwriter, is first. She wrote: *A man and a woman meet in a book-filled room but the woman doesn't like the man. When the woman sees the man approach, she leaves. The man likes the woman and doesn't understand. When he sees that she left her backpack, he picks it up and goes to find her.*

Yin treats it like a blog, which fits with her work: *Another day in a nearly empty study hall. One student leaves, another comes in. The bell rings, and he leaves.* I wonder if Professor Forsythe sees how little Yin got from the video. I hope so.

Peggy, who wants to be a lawyer, has a different take: *A high school girl leaves her backpack in the cafeteria. A thuggish guy comes in from outside and steals her backpack.*

Keisha, the historical novelist wrote: *This is a transitional scene where two lovers fail to connect. Clearly, the girl and the guy have had some type of disagreement and are trying to avoid each other. The girl, seeing that the guy is coming, leaves so she doesn't have to see him. He's relieved that she's not there.*

I go next, and then Tess is last. I'm very curious to hear what she wrote. I wonder if she'll embellish the scene since she writes fan fiction. She reads aloud, *A young woman is sitting at a table in a room which could be a conference room, some type of lobby, or a large schoolroom. She stands up and walks offscreen to the left, as if she were leaving or going to another area of the room. Another person walks in from the right. The person could be a man or a woman. The person sees a bag on the floor, which might belong either to the young woman or this second person. The person looks around, perhaps for the young woman, then walks off to the right.*

Interesting. Tess sounds unsure of what she saw. If she's going into the military, I thought she would show more certainty. Also, there's nothing fanciful about what she wrote. I'd have thought a writer of fan fiction based on a TV show about witches would see magic or dragons or something.

Professor Forsythe asks us to review our own pieces and see if we have any changes based on what we heard from each other. I don't have any. I know what I saw and I didn't put in any extra details. No one else makes any changes either.

Professor Forsythe says, "Well, that means that you differ on material facts, doesn't it? It also means that each of you has made assumptions which are incorrect. Take another look and see if you can identify your assumptions."

She's right. We all did make assumptions, and they are different! Professor Forsythe leads a discussion in which we go through them. As we do, she writes on a whiteboard:

1. *Where did this take place?*
2. *What was the first person doing at the beginning?*
3. *What did she do next?*
3. *What is the second person's description?*
4. *What is the relationship between the two people?*
5. *What was the second person doing there?*
6. *What did the second person walk out with? Why?*

I wish I could figure out the point of all of this, because obviously Professor Forsythe is looking for something specific. The only good news is, I don't think Yin has any more of a clue what the Professor wants than I do.

Professor Forsythe puts down the marker. "Let's play it again."

Each of us was wrong in a million different ways. It was not a second girl, but a guy, so Peggy, Keisha, Yin, and I got that wrong. I thought the room had bookshelves in the back, but there were only a couple of books on the tables and no shelves. I was right that it was a messenger bag. When we see the whole thing again, it's clear that the girl didn't sit anywhere near the bag, so it couldn't have been hers. No bell went off, so she didn't get up because study hall ended as Yin thought. Finally, the guy smiled a little when he picked up the bag and left. He didn't shrug. So much for making "an excellent impression" on Professor Forsythe this time. Tess was the closest, but she also bought herself the most wiggle room by putting in multiple possibilities.

When the video is over, Professor Forsythe asks us, "Do you know why this exercise is called 'Show and Tell?'"

Yin answers, "Because you're showing us something and asking us to tell about it."

"Close, Yin, but not quite. Anyone else?"

I raise my hand, and Professor Forsythe nods at me. "What we've written shows and tells something about us?"

"Yes, Soph, correct." Hah! I got the answer before Yin did! *And* she finally got my name right.

Professor Forsythe keeps talking. "Each of your assumptions says something about you. So do the assumptions you did not make. And for Tess here, the assumptions she implied but refused to make. Now I don't know you very well, but I'm going to make a statement about each one of you and I want you to think about whether I'm right or not."

"First, Soph: School is very important to you, and you work hard at it. You have a lot of friends and are devoted to them, but you have strong opinions about how they should act. In fact, you have strong opinions about a lot of things. But you're generous, too. Am I right? Does anyone know why I came to these conclusions?"

She *is* right, and I have to admit it, but I wonder how she figured it out. At least she didn't say anything bad about me.

Ellen guesses, "Well, for one thing, she said it was a school and she assumed the girl and the guy knew each other and were supposed to be there together."

Peggy agrees and adds, "Also, you think they were supposed to be there together but the girl ditched the guy."

Ellen has more. "You said that they were supposed to meet but that the girl blew off the guy. Actually, you said they were both girls. Then when the guy couldn't find the girl, he shrugged as if he knew she was wrong to leave."

Professor Forsythe describes the others, but I don't pay much attention. I think my memory is great. Also, I may have strong opinions, but I'm perceptive, not judgmental. I don't think there's anything wrong with that. I still wonder how I got so many details wrong. I guess I should be grateful Professor Forsythe got my name right this time.

We go through everyone's answers but I'm so distracted by how Professor Forsythe figured me out that I don't really pay attention until I hear her describe Tess. "You are an extremely careful person. You're careful about what you say and do and you're concerned about being judged by others. You're very observant, but you keep your own counsel." She looks around the room and continues. "What in Tessa's writing suggests this?"

I correct her. "Her name is Tess, not Tessa." I wonder if Professor Forsythe is as perceptive as she thinks she is. I realize too late I probably shouldn't have corrected her. I can't keep arguing with her. From rooming with Tess, I know some of what Professor Forsythe said is right. The rest is intriguing, and I wonder if it's true.

Professor Forsythe tells Yin she has a creative voice but needs encouragement to share her talents. "But you're working hard," she says, smiling.

Great. Another point for Yin. She hasn't corrected Professor Forsythe once.

✳   ✳   ✳

AT THE END OF LUNCH, Joan stands up. I guess Professor Forsythe is taking a break from playing the announcer. Joan says that we will devote the afternoon to individual writing instruction. "After carefully reviewing your applications and listening to you over the last twenty-four hours, we've assigned each of you to work with one of us. Our goal is to help you define your objectives and help you to realize them. We're going to post a list in the lounge which identifies which instructor is paired with which writer and schedules a time for each of you to meet one-on-one with your instructor today. You should find your instructor and your appointment and then pick a place to write for the rest of the afternoon. We'll be conducting our meetings in the large conference room. You can work in your own bedrooms, in any of the public spaces, or in the smaller rooms on the third floor."

Excellent! I'm sure I'll be paired with Professor Forsythe, since she's a poetry expert. I can't wait to show her what I am working on and finally ask for her insight. Maybe I do have a shot at Minerva. If nothing else, I now have something to tell my mother that has nothing to do with the stupid deb ball. I join the crowd at the list on the bulletin board and push my way to the front.

I can't find my name on Professor Forsythe's list. Tess *is* on her list. That makes no sense, since Professor Forsythe clearly doesn't know anything about fan fiction. I am assigned to Grace. That sucks. She's the youngest one here and isn't even affiliated with Minerva. I'm the first one on her list and have to meet with her right away, which leaves me no time to figure out how to approach Professor Forsythe about this.

Each of the four instructors sits at a corner of the conference room table. Professor Forsythe is already talking to Yin. That figures! I sit at Grace's corner, shaking my head.

"Hi, Soph. Let's talk about your work. I see you're a poet and you write historical poems?" Her voice goes up a little at the end, as if she's one of those West Coast girls on TV, making a statement into a question.

"No, not quite." I get it now. They mistook my interest in historical structures for poems about history, which must be why they didn't assign me to Professor Forsythe. "I do write poetry, but I'm interested in sonnets. I've been working on the simpler types, you know, with couplets, but I want to be able to do the more complicated rhyme schemes."

"Ah, I see. Tell me what you write about?"

"Everything. I mean, everything that's going on around me. Sometimes about how I'm feeling. Other times about what I see: right and wrong, that type of thing."

"How do you decide what to write about?"

"I don't. I write… whatever hits me. It's the form that I think about all the time."

"Show me what you're working on now?"

I take out my sonnet about coming here. "This one is a Shakespearean structure—the first one I did which wasn't just couplets." I watch her read it.

"Yes, I see, ABAB. So, you want to write more of these?"

"Sort of. I want to write ABAB. But I also want to be able to write Petrarchan and Spenserian." Those are pretty complicated poetry structures. I assume Professor Forsythe would know them, but I can't tell if Grace does. She nods.

"And those formats are important to you because?"

This seems like a waste of time. Grace turns everything I say into another dumb question. "I love them. They were developed hundreds of years ago, and everything should still be able to fit into them. I like ordering my thoughts to fit into them. I like being who I am in the twenty-first century, but using an historic construct. It's traditional but updated, which is more sophisticated."

"Huh." She's still nodding, but I don't think she knows what I'm talking about.

We go back and forth like this, and Grace suggests I consider what "comes next?" I think she means I should do something else, but I do not intend to do that. "You should think about how what you want to say about yourself fits into the form and whether the form should be updated."

On my way out, I notice that Professor Forsythe has finished with Yin and I try to catch her eye, but she's focused on the papers in front of her.

Tess.

I DON'T KNOW WHY PROFESSOR Forsythe chose me. Yesterday, I thought she didn't like fan fiction at all—or me. In the hour before I have to go meet with her, I retreat to our room to think up a defense for what I write. I'm trying to read my latest chapter on my tiny phone screen, and am pretty frustrated, when Soph comes in. I politely ask how it went, but she glowers at me as if I did something to her and says nothing.

"That bad?" I can't figure out what she might be upset about.

"Professor Forsythe should have been mine; she's a poetry expert. But I got Grace instead, who just picked me apart. You're lucky you got Professor Forsythe. That's a big honor."

It doesn't feel like much of an honor, but I don't want to argue with Soph. I also don't want to explain what I saw last night between Chris and Orly. I have my own problems.

"Was Grace mean?" That's a bad sign. If Grace was mean to Soph, Professor Forsythe will almost certainly be worse to me. This week is getting harder and harder. I don't know why they chose me. Some of these girls have been published or won awards for their writing. I'm putting things online that aren't edited and that no one even knows I wrote. They're taken from a TV show that Professor Forsythe doesn't watch. At least Soph has a poet for an instructor. There's no "fan fiction professor" here for me to talk to. Soph is still glum.

"Worse. She didn't say anything outright, but she questioned everything I told her, as though she didn't buy any of it. What a pain! I don't think she understands structured poetry at all."

"What are you going to do?" Soph doesn't strike me as someone who just accepts things. She's probably going to make a fuss.

"I'm not sure. I want to talk to Professor Forsythe and see if I can change. It must be a mistake."

"You can have my spot, if you want it."

Soph perks up when I say that. "I can?"

I say, "Yes," without thinking.

"When are you supposed to meet with her?" She's got a glint in her eye as if I offered her something important. Maybe I did. Maybe it will save me from being critiqued even more and keep some distance between Professor Forsythe and me. I don't care who my advisor is. I want to make it through this week without more humiliation and go home.

"In a few minutes," I tell her.

"Great. I'll come down with you, and we'll work it out." She's a lot happier now. Better for Soph to ask to switch anyway. Again, I think maybe Soph and I could be friends.

We go down to the conference room. Professor Forsythe is distracted. "Good afternoon, Tess." She turns to Soph, "And Ms., um, why are you here?" Great, she can't remember Soph's name *again*.

"Professor, we think there's been a mistake, that I should be working with you, not Tess."

"And why is that?" She's clearly not happy. *I* didn't think that it was a mistake. Soph did, and I don't want her putting words in my mouth. But it's too late. Soph is already explaining.

"Because I'm a perfect match for you. I'm a poet, which is your specialty, and I am working in pre-twentieth-century structures, exactly what you're working on in your current project. I meant it when I said I want to work with you." Soph is almost pleading.

Professor Forsythe gazes back and forth between us without speaking. I haven't said anything, and I feel Soph nudging me. "It's fine with me if Soph wants to switch, ma'am."

"Well, Soph, I may be flattered by your interest." She doesn't sound flattered at all. "But I assure you, there's been no mistake. We assigned you to work with Grace. I am confident that when you meet with her, you'll understand and appreciate our decision."

Soph looks as though she's about to say something more, but nothing comes out. That's a relief.

"Now, please leave Tess and me so that we can discuss her work. If you want to talk to me about your work, we will have an opportunity later this week."

Once Soph leaves the room, Professor Forsythe turns to me with one eyebrow raised. "Before we start, Tess, do you have a problem here?"

"No, no." I rush to assure her. "I… It was important to her… but no."

"Good. Now let's talk about your fan fiction." To my relief, she doesn't say it with the same emphasis she used yesterday morning. "I have read some of it and I listened to you talk about it yesterday. I appreciate that you want to use it to demonstrate women's inherent power, but I think you should try to put more of your personal experience into it."

"Well… the show is set in an alternate world with magic." I don't know how to explain that the whole point of writing fan fiction is that it's set in a place and time that aren't real, that have absolutely nothing to do with my puny, pathetic existence in Castleton, New Hampshire.

"Yes, as I say, I did read it, both when you submitted a writing sample with your application and more recently. Your writing technique is very competent. But there's not much of *you* in here, Tess. Even if you try to address it through one of the show's characters, I'd like to see some of your own feelings and hopes, as well as your personal history."

I'm slightly sick to my stomach as I leave. There's no way that I can do what she wants. And there's no way I can tell her why I can't.

✳ ✳ ✳

From Soph Alcazar's Writing Journal,
February 12, 2018

Two chances to shine and I failed outright.
Shone but shown up to the wrong one assigned.

Chapter Ten

From the Fan Fiction Unbound Archive,
posted by con Tessaofthecastle:

The rain battered them ferociously. From the way the wind was howling, Daphne could tell that the storm wasn't going to let up anytime soon. They had to get to shelter. Behind Daphne, Astoria whimpered with fear.

Soph.

ALL I CAN THINK ABOUT is how Professor Forsythe probably won't even talk to me for the rest of the week. Tess is in trouble too, and Grace didn't help me at all. I spend the rest of the afternoon alone in a little room on the third floor, trying to diagram the sonnet forms, but the words won't come. What a disaster this is turning out to be! I will probably never get into Minerva. And I'll be lucky if I don't have to repeat senior year at some boarding school in Switzerland.

Tess and I barely talk to each other in our room before we go down to dinner. I'm curious how it went with the two of them, but I'm not going to ask. It will only aggravate me. At dinner, I try to sit as far away from Professor Forsythe, Grace, and Tess as possible.

After the meal is over, Professor Forsythe stands up. "Well, thanks to Yin and Clover for that delicious chicken pot pie." She nods at them. "Part of the tradition of this conference is that we flip the lights on in the courtyard and everyone pairs up to make snowsisters. This is a conference for young women, so we don't make snowmen. We make snow women, in a half circle facing the lounge windows. Each of you should find someone to work with. Why don't you put on your coats and boots and then come back down and meet in the lounge to choose a partner. We'll pass out things for eyes, mouths, and other features."

Back in our room, Tess asks, "Where are your boots?"

"Right here. I'm putting them on."

"No, I mean your snow boots. Don't you have duck boots or something?"

"These Chloés will be fine. I wear them everywhere."

Tess seems doubtful, but doesn't say anything. We put on jackets, hats, gloves, and scarves. Then we go downstairs again in silence.

I'm about to ask Clover to be my partner, but when Tess and I step into the lounge, I see Orly standing all alone, wrapped in her maroon coat, shivering slightly, so I go up to her. "Want to partner with me, Orly?"

She looks startled but relieved. Her eyes dart around the room over my head, and I don't understand why.

She smiles and says, "Definitely."

Tess.

BETWEEN PROFESSOR FORSYTHE'S INSISTENCE THAT I put myself into *The Witches' Circle* and the tension in our group project, I wouldn't mind pulling the covers over my head and skipping the evening activity. Soph's silence doesn't help.

I find myself thinking again about Chris. I don't think Chris should be writing secretly about Orly. On the other hand, I don't want to rat her out. I'm not comfortable with whispering to her about it and I really don't want to be involved in any controversy. I've already irritated Professor Forsythe. It's hard enough figuring out the writing parts of this conference without having to get personal or explain *why* I can't get personal. If this conference was my big chance to show anyone outside of Castleton what I can do, I'm blowing it.

I manage to sit by Gabriela and Keisha at the other end of the dinner table from Chris, which is a relief. Chris sits with Janaye and Yin. Orly is in the middle of the table, and Yin almost sits next to her. But when she sees Chris, she moves over, leaving an empty space next to Orly.

Gabriela's nice, and I relax a bit, talking to her and Keisha. Soph talks to her about poetry. Out of the corner of my eye, I keep watching Soph. Something about her is fascinating. She's one of those girls who is immediately the center of attention, even in a group of people who hadn't met before. She's loud and funny and she talks a lot. She's always pushing that long, black hair behind her ears, and I would be completely intimidated by her except she's so friendly that she isn't intimidating any more. She reminds me of Daphne, the character on *The Witches' Circle*, who is beautiful and kind and draws people to her with her magic, only Soph is not quite as wise as Daphne.

I push chicken and peas around my plate while I listen to Soph ask everyone questions about their writing. She leans toward

Orly and asks her about living in the South. She's friendly about it, unlike Chris.

"Is it totally different up here?"

"Yes. We don't have snow like this. And everything's so spread out here, just woods for miles. I haven't seen any fast food places or strip malls like we have at home."

"But, I mean, do *we* seem different? Other than our accents"

"I don't mind people being different. But y'all do talk very fast, hon. Butter's not gonna melt in your mouth!" She laughs. "My Meemaw would never let me talk so fast. She'd tell you, 'Soph, child, the Good Lord only gave me two ears. I can't hear as fast as you're speaking.'" Soph laughs at her impression.

After dinner, when we pair up, I think maybe I'll ask to build a snowsister with Soph, to try to mend fences, but Clover slips in front of me at the door, and I can hear them talking as we go outside. Clover asks Soph if she has a boyfriend.

Soph laughs, a bright, high-pitched giggle, and says, "Not on that team. I like girls."

I'm startled, as I was at the pizza place, hearing her say it right out loud. I'm not sure how I feel about it. But it makes me head in the other direction, toward Gabriela, and the two of us push wet snow together to make a base. Soph ends up with Orly, and Clover pairs up with someone else. Keisha wanders back toward Chris, and they invite Yin to work with them.

It's snowing, the heavy, soft, wet kind, in big flakes, which is perfect for snowsisters. I like that word. No one at home would ever think to say it. Gabriela and I work together pretty well. I can hear other groups talking as they work on their sculptures. Chris and Keisha and some of the girls I haven't met yet are all talking to each other in low voices by their snowsisters. I wonder if Chris is telling them about my writing, because one of the other girls shakes her head in disgust and rolls her eyes.

I hear Soph laugh and I look over at her and Orly. Soph must have gone up to the room and brought back a bra. It's got to be hers, all black and lacy. She and Orly are laughing, trying to figure out how to fasten it around their snowsister. It's clever. It's also not something I would ever dare do, in part because my bras come from JC Penney and they aren't that pretty.

Yin comes over to us, carrying a bucket of carrots and rocks for eyes and buttons. I'm reaching in to pick out rocks that will work when she leans toward us. She says, "Hey, Orly's not really a girl."

I stiffen. Chris is obviously talking to everyone about Orly.

Gabriela asks Yin what she means, and she pulls us into a tight circle. "Chris found out Orly's trans. He's really a boy, but he's trying to become a girl. I'm not sure Chris is safe staying in the same room with him. I think we should say something. Stand up for her."

Gabriela asks, "How does Chris even know something like that?"

Yin shrugs. "She says she can prove it. But I told her she should go to the professors. I told her I'd go with her."

My breath catches in my throat. This is not something I want any part of, but I wonder what my dad would say. Standing up for Chris would certainly count as leadership, if she genuinely thinks she's unsafe. I see Orly and Soph still fiddling with the black bra. Orly flashes a weak smile in my direction.

Gabriela says, "Stand up for Chris or Orly? If you mean Chris, I'm pretty sure it will be fine. I mean, I've never met any trans people, but I don't see a problem. He—I mean she—is here as a girl, right? So, I doubt she wants to cause trouble with her roommate."

She makes a good point. This is why I can't figure out how to be a leader. I'm always thinking about both sides.

Yin stares at her, then says, "Well, some of us are going to say something. I mean women have to stick up for each other, right? She nods in my direction. "Right, Tess?"

I mumble, "I don't know. I'll think about it." I still want to stay out of it.

We all admire the completed snowsisters. Some have scarves and hats. Most have breasts, of varying sizes and shapes. We take selfies and a group photo. Yin and Chris are standing by their snowsister. They ask Soph to come stand with them and she does, slinging a casual arm around Yin's shoulder. I don't know how she is so comfortable with people she just met. I don't know if she heard what Chris and Yin have been saying.

As we go back inside, everyone stomps their feet to shake the snow off. I look up at the sky again. The snow isn't letting up. It will probably fall all night.

Up in our room, Soph peels off her suede boots. As I suspected, they are completely soaked through.

"Ugh," she says, "these are a mess." She tosses them into a corner. "My feet are freezing cold." She rummages through her bag for a pair of socks. She looks up, frustrated. "I didn't check my bag after Betty packed it. I can't find any other socks."

"Do you want to borrow some?" I rummage through my bag and pull out a pair of pink and gray fleece socks. They are the warmest ones I own. Her face brightens, and she takes them from me. "Thanks," she says. "Pink isn't my favorite color, but they're thick enough."

"What will you wear tomorrow?" I ask, worried. The snow isn't going to stop, and she said those were her only boots. "I don't have any other boots with me and I don't think we wear the same size anyway."

She stops pulling on my socks. They look slightly out of place on her graceful little white feet under her trendy skinny jeans. She shrugs, then says, "Don't worry Tess, I can manage."

Okay, not my problem. She changes the subject. "You know, Yin and Chris are going around complaining about Orly being trans." So, they got to her, too.

"I know." I don't say anything else.

"Well?" She has a slightly exasperated expression.

"Well, what?" I say. This is not a conversation I want to have. I don't mention what Chris said about trying to investigate Orly or overhearing her asking Orly questions downstairs.

"Well," she repeats, speaking slowly, as though I'm a child. "Don't you think we need to speak up for Orly? I mean, they're being completely unfair to her."

"Is she really… like, trans?" I ask.

"Yeah. You know what that means, right?"

That makes me mad. "Yes, Soph. I know what 'trans' means. We know a *few* things in New Hampshire." She doesn't pay attention to the sarcasm in my voice.

"She told me. I think she's nervous about being here."

"Well, maybe she should try to switch roommates and keep quiet." I shrug. I don't want to get into this. But maybe getting Orly to switch rooms would solve all the problems.

Soph's eyes flash. "You know, Tess, she shouldn't have to speak up or keep quiet about who she is. And she certainly shouldn't have to change who she is for anyone. Chris and Yin are the ones forcing the issue, which shouldn't be an issue anyway."

I don't say anything.

"Shouldn't Orly be able to attend this conference like every other girl here? She hasn't done anything wrong." She shakes her head in frustration. "Boy, I was hoping someone would back me up on this. I backed you up with Professor Forsythe about your writing. I'm supposed to be trying to impress her."

She's right about that. I take a deep breath.

"Look," I say, "I don't want any trouble. I don't want to get involved." And I mean that. This conference is a real opportunity for me, and I might not have another. My West Point panel interview is coming up, and I don't want to take any chances with that. One thing I definitely learned growing up in Castleton is that you keep certain things to yourself. But I can hear my father's voice and I don't know the right thing to do.

"Fine." She's mad. I can tell. "Understood. I'm going down for hot chocolate. Maybe we need some of this." She reaches into her knapsack and pulls out a heavy-looking bottle of dark alcohol. She notices me staring. "It's only Hennessy. We're not children, Tess."

"Soph, all the chaperones are going to be there. Do you think now's the time for that?"

She wavers and then puts the bottle back into her knapsack. I hear a chirp and see her take out her phone. "Oh, God, not Mom again," she says to herself. Then she walks out of the room without another word, still wearing my pink and gray socks.

* * *

From Soph Alcazar's Writing Journal,
February 12, 2018

Right, wrong, the difference I think I know.
How can they punish her, even in snow?

Chapter Eleven

From the Fan Fiction Unbound Archive,
posted by conTessaofthecastle:

Outside, rain continued to fall. They huddled together in the small cave. It had been pouring for hours. "Aren't you tired of this?" asked Daphne.

Astoria leaned up against her, fiddling with a bit of twine in her hands. She was braiding and knotting what appeared to be a bracelet or an anklet. "No," she said simply, and Daphne was surprised by how calm her voice was. "I didn't like being out in the rain. But this is fine. It's better than being at home, fearing for my safety from Lord Quintana and his minions."

Lightning struck a tree nearby.

Soph.

I'M PISSED OFF BY THE injustice here. Yin and Chris want to punish Orly and say that she's not really a girl. They keep talking about "safety," but that's bullshit, like my mother's constant warnings. I don't get Tess either. I don't think she likes what Yin and Chris are doing, but she doesn't care enough to say anything. Total buzzkill on the alcohol, but she is right about the chaperones; I go down for hot chocolate and cookies and to find Orly or Gabriela, but neither of them is there and I don't see Professor Forsythe so I don't stay. I can't be bothered to talk to Grace.

When I go back to the room, Tess is asleep, or pretending to be. I text my friends,

[FROM SOPH TO GORDON, LALLY, AND MIBS] *Transphobes in NH 2night!*

[FROM LALLY TO GORDON, MIBS, AND SOPH] *What's up?*

[FROM SOPH TO GORDON, LALLY, AND MIBS] *One of us is trans. These people R freaking.*

[FROM MIBS TO GORDON, LALLY, AND SOPH] *WTF?*

[FROM SOPH TO GORDON, LALLY, AND MIBS] *I know, right? Tiny minds.*

[FROM GORDON TO LALLY, MIBS, AND SOPH] *Wuts she like?*

[FROM SOPH TO GORDON, LALLY, AND MIBS] *She's nice! She wants to be here like everyone else.*

[FROM LALLY TO GORDON, MIBS, AND SOPH] *R U going to do anything?*

[FROM SOPH TO GORDON, LALLY, AND MIBS] *I don't know. I don't want to make a bigger deal out of it.*

[FROM MIBS TO GORDON, LALLY, AND SOPH] *You have to stick up for her.*

This is why we all love Mibs. She's all peace and social justice, like her uncle.

[FROM LALLY TO GORDON, MIBS, AND SOPH] *What are they doing 2 her?*

I think about it.

[FROM SOPH TO GORDON, LALLY, AND MIBS] *Talking about her behind her back so far. But she knows.*

Mibs is smart about these things.

[From Mibs to Gordon, Lally, and Soph] *Tell them to stop. If you like her, hang out.*

She's right. If I make a big deal about it, it might be worse for Orly. Maybe it will blow over.

[From Soph to Gordon, Lally, and Mibs] *Thx. Later.*

I struggle to fall asleep. I thought this week was going to be fun and help me get into college at the same time. But I didn't count on being assigned to the wrong instructor or Professor Forsythe not liking me. I figured people would be too cool to split over something like the thing with Orly. Now I'm stuck with a roommate who's so timid she will barely say her own name and I may have to leave the whole week out of my Common App.

Tess.

The next morning while we're dressing, Soph and I are that kind of stiff-polite people get when they're both mad but trying not to show it. I finally get a text back from Joey.

[From Joey to Tess] *Stay safe.*

It makes me feel better. Soph notices me on my phone and asks, "Boyfriend again?" I nod, silently. I notice she's still wearing my socks when we go to breakfast. Her ruined boots are lying in the corner of the room.

We spend the morning doing individual work and meeting with our assigned instructors. Professor Forsythe pulls me aside to ask if I thought about what she said yesterday, and I tell her I have, but that I don't really know how to do it. I think she might hear the frustration in my voice, because she's friendlier.

"Tess, the committee thought the chapter you submitted with your application was very good. I don't watch the television show, but the dialogue you drafted gave a strong sense of the characters. We thought the substance showed promise as well. When I say that I want to see more of you in there, I mean to encourage someone who has an interesting life to write about it. I'd like to know her better through her fiction."

"Thank you," I mumble. Then I catch myself and stand up straight. "Yes, ma'am."

"I also think you are building something here, but you haven't figured out where it will go. If you concentrate on what you know best about yourself, you'll find it. Trust me."

There's no way I'm going to share any details of my "interesting life" on a dairy farm, but we talk about the show and how the season is shaping up. I feel funny talking to an adult about fictional characters on TV as if they're real people. When I say that to her, Professor Forsythe says, "Just because they're fictional doesn't mean they aren't important. Let's think of fictional characters we've both read."

We come up with Scout from *To Kill a Mockingbird* and Celie from *The Color Purple*.

"You see, Tess, these fictional characters with problems, weaknesses, and bad habits, they teach us a lot, and we can think about what they would do when we struggle to solve our own problems. They can be as real as you and I. Harper Lee and Alice Walker would both tell you that they put parts of themselves into those characters. Readers and fans don't want their characters to be perfect. The writing makes them real, because the writers know who they are. Daphne and Astoria are young women—such as yourself. You want to put them in situations where they learn to use the powers that you think they have but haven't accessed. You have powers like that too, don't you think?"

I don't think I have any power, and I'm definitely not Alice Walker. But I feel better about Professor Forsythe. She's strict, but she must be a good teacher. I'm glad she doesn't think my writing is worthless. I'm still not exactly sure how my story is going to end, but I sketch out a couple of ideas and figure if I keep writing, something will make sense. One thing I do know: I don't have to post anything I write here if I don't like it. I'm still anonymous online.

Before I leave the session, I ask something I've been wondering about. "Is it true that you'll meet with us privately? Not just in the group sessions?"

She cocks her head as though she doesn't understand my question. "Tess, this is what this conference is for. To give everyone a chance not only to work with their peers, but to seek out extra guidance when they need it. We're all here because we're teachers, and we know students learn in different ways. Sometimes people are more comfortable sharing things one-on-one."

"I didn't know we could do that."

"If you always wait for permission, you will miss out on many things in life," she says, but she's smiling at me as I leave.

Snowsisters

* * *

From Soph Alcazar's Writing Journal,
February 13, 2018

A week in a place with people unfair.
I cannot understand why they don't care.

Chapter Twelve

From the Fan Fiction Unbound Archive,
posted by conTessaofthecastle:

The rain lasted all night. Daphne and Astoria slept fitfully,
waking each other with every movement. The next morning
was damp, but the rain had stopped. They started walking
early, eager to leave the cramped cave. Water dripped from
trees as they started off through the forest. Daphne was worried
about making up for the time they got lost during the storm.
Lord Quintana's harridans must be using powerful seeking
spells, which would find them eventually. She walked more
quickly. Astoria wordlessly kept pace.

Soph.

FOR OUR INDIVIDUAL PROJECTS, THEY tell us we can work wherever
we want, including the rooms on the third floor. No one is staying
up there, but they opened the rooms in case we want to work
alone or with someone else, away from the others. We're supposed
to tell the instructors where we are so they can check in on us
and talk about what we're doing.

Yin surprises me by inviting me to go up there and work with
her. I'm still pissed about the Orly thing, but I need to find a way
to impress Professor Forsythe. Yin must know her more than she

would admit at pizza the other night, since they're on a first-name basis. We go up the stairs with a few other girls, including Tess.

Yin asks, "Soph, why sonnets?"

I feel as if I've been answering this for years. "I like the tradition and the challenge of organizing my thoughts and feelings. I like the setup, the argument, and the resolution. I like the sensation that I am doing something great poets have been doing for centuries. I like to write in a style I wouldn't use when I speak to you."

At the top of the stairs, I see the rooms are smaller than ours. Yin and I choose one and sit on the floor, leaning against the bed.

I continue, "Also, I like the format, but I want to use it to communicate ideas that never would have been in sonnets when they were developed, like social issues, not love and flowers and pretty things."

Now I ask Yin, "Why free verse?"

"I like the freedom of it, working out how words sound without forcing them into a rhyme or a pattern someone's done before," she says matter-of-factly. "But I'm interested in something more tightly composed. I thought we could work together. I'd like to see how you do it."

I'm flattered and a little intimidated. I don't have much of a method. I think about what's going on and then fill in the structure. When I explain it to her, she says it's not that different from what she does. So, I take out my laptop and show her, using a spreadsheet with the fourteen ten-syllable lines, in an ABAB CDCD EFEF GG pattern, all set up.

"What do you want to write about?" I ask.

She tells me about stuff that's going on at her school: a fight over whether a teacher should stay. The kids like him, but the parents don't. We shoot ideas back and forth, putting the kids' feelings in the first stanza, then the adults' in the next, then the conflict in the third and, finally, a couplet resolving it. Yin wants to do it without rhyming. That doesn't sound right to me. A sonnet has traditional rules: fourteen lines of ten syllables each, with a specific rhyme scheme.

Yin asks, "Who's your instructor? I've got Joan."

"I thought you had Prof—Helen!"

"No, Joan. Why did you think I had Helen?"

"I saw you talking with her when I went in to talk to Grace."

"Oh. I was trying to switch my night to make dinner so I can cook with Chris."

She tells me I'm lucky I got Grace. I ask why, swallowing my objection to Chris.

"Because she writes poetry herself. She's some kind of prodigy. I think she's one of those people who can make it up on the spot and it always rhymes, with perfect meter. Why—don't you like her?"

I explain that I had hoped to work with Professor Forsythe since she knows all about the structures that interest me, leaving out that it would be good for college admissions.

Yin says she thinks "Helen" is too stiff. "Helen contacted me after I got this New York State Teachers' grant for new media last year. She called my high school about it and wanted me to apply for this conference. But she's been totally distant so far this week." So much for getting anything helpful from Yin.

I'm about to confront her about Orly when Joan pokes her head in. "Hi, how's it going?"

We explain where we are. I tell her that sonnets have a complex rhyming scheme that makes them sonnets, and Joan says, "Soph, what's wrong with playing a little bit with the piece? Yin wants shape, but not necessarily rules. Let her try that and then listen to it. Maybe you want to try something more like free verse yourself. You're here to do something new, right?"

"I *do* want to do something new. I want to try a more complicated structure," I protest.

"What's more complicated than no set structure?"

Tess.

PROFESSOR FORSYTHE TELLS ME DESKTOP computers are available in the third-floor writing rooms, and I go up there to work on my latest chapter before lunch. Soph is talking to Yin down the hall, and I wonder if they're discussing Orly. I'm trying to figure out how to put some of myself in the story, but for some reason all I can think of is Angie. I know I can't put a cow into a story about witches, but I wonder how she's doing. I text Mom to ask. She tells me that the calf is still bottle-feeding, and is growing. Then she tells me that Daddy said if she is still doing all right when the conference is over I can name her. That's how I know he's forgiven me.

I text Joey and tell him what Professor Forsythe said about my writing.

He sends a reply almost immediately, so he's bored.

[FROM JOEY TO TESS] *You're going to have to figure out how to talk about yourself sometime, Tess. Might as well start now.*

I put my phone down and sigh. Things might be better at home, but I still don't understand these girls at all. Keisha is the only one I've met who understands what I write. Professor Forsythe is pushing me to write things I never thought I could put on paper. Chris and Orly are confusing me in ways I don't know how to figure out. And Soph… Well, Soph is so many different things I can't begin to count them. She's smart and funny and clever. She knows about all kinds of things I don't: how to use a subway, how to get girls to flock to her like a celebrity. But she doesn't seem to know how to convince Professor Forsythe to like her, or how to solve the problems between Chris and Orly. She did offer to help me write poetry for my spells. Maybe if we work together I can figure out the rest of it.

Joey's text is stuck in my head: "Might as well start now." But so are Daddy's words, "Make us proud, Tess." I don't know who to listen to, and the more I try to figure it out, the more confused I end up.

I stare blankly at my computer screen. Daphne and Astoria are stuck in the woods, wet and scared, with no clear way to shelter. Maybe if I make one of them do something totally unexpected, that will point me in a new direction.

⁂ ⁂ ⁂

From Soph Alcazar's Writing Journal,
February 13, 2018

Structure, rhyme scheme, meter, all in my lane.
But here they tell me no, confusion reigns.

Chapter Thirteen

From the Fan Fiction Unbound Archive,
posted by conTessaofthecastle:

Daphne walked even faster, concentrating on the space-shifting spell. She could sense Astoria right behind her. As Daphne carefully uttered the incantation, focused only on the sensation in her fingertips and the Portal of Arden, Astoria stumbled on a tree root and fell toward her. Daphne didn't see it, but as soon as Astoria grabbed Daphne's arm to keep herself from falling, Daphne felt a surge of power through her hands. She heard Astoria gasp. A gust of air swirled around them. When she opened her eyes, Astoria was gone. Daphne stood alone in the forest.

Daphne closed her eyes, trying to focus on what she had done differently when she cast the spell this time. She had been saying the words when suddenly Astoria touched her arm. Something changed when Astoria touched her that made the spell take effect.

Soph.

THIS AFTERNOON, WE PUT AWAY the laptops—Celestine tells us, "Put your quills down"—and go skating. I was hoping for this and, luckily, Betty packed my Jacksons, which are in the bottom of my bag. When I pull them out in our room, Tess knits her brow.

"What?"

"Nothing, Soph. I didn't know we were supposed to bring skates. They usually provide them." She pulls on thick socks, almost as thick as the ones she lent me.

Uh oh. Maybe I'll be the only one. Well, whatever. These skates fit me perfectly, so I'm bringing them. I haven't skated at all this winter, much to Mom's chagrin. I've been doing it since I was a kid in the Alps, when Mom and Papa skied down slopes much too dangerous for me. In the middle grades, it was my chosen winter sport at Partridge, but then I got to the upper school and could just take gym and do other extracurrics, like the literary magazine. I also gave up skating because Mom wanted me to compete and offered to buy me sparkly, short dresses and feathered headpieces. No thanks.

We walk out of the lodge in a big group to a yellow school bus waiting in the driveway. Tess was right. No one else is carrying skates. I see Orly take a window seat and sit next to her. I'm feeling protective of Orly. Chris, Yin, and Keisha are all sitting together. Tess goes past them and sits with Gabriela.

I ask, "Do you like skating, Orly?"

She turns her head from the window, and it's obviously an effort for her to respond. "Never done it, Soph. They probably don't have any skates big enough for me anyway."

"Oh, skating is fun, Orly. I hope you'll come out with me." She frowns.

"Try not to think about it too hard. It's like dancing; once you try it, you can't stop. I almost wish I still did it for school."

"Okay, Soph. Thank you."

I settle in the seat right next to her with our shoulders touching, and we ride in silence.

After about twenty minutes, the bus pulls into a small parking lot, and I see a little building and a frozen pond. The sun is out now, and part of the pond has been cleared for skating. A path leads through the snow from the parking lot to the building, and another connects the building to the pond. Everyone goes into the building, where there are dozens of pairs of skates for men and women.

I see Orly linger in the doorway and motion to her. She bites her lip, saying, "I don't see any that are likely to fit me, Soph." She tells me her size in a small voice.

"I'll find you a pair. Have a seat on the bench, and I'll be right over." I have no trouble finding her a pair. She stares at me, doubt still clouding her face as I sit on the bench. "Give me a minute to lace up, and I'll help you with yours."

Orly sighs as if she's very unhappy, but when I kneel in front of her to lace up her skates, her eyes are friendly. "Thanks, Soph. You're a peach."

I stand and reach out my hand. "Come on, let's go down to the pond. You don't have to skate, but you might want to try it. I promise it's something you'll never forget." She stands gingerly, and we walk down with everyone else. My breath is like smoke. I usually skate on indoor rinks, where it's warmer. The ice is rougher than at a rink, but there's a lot of room to build up speed.

There are plastic deck chairs and wooden benches at the edges of the skating area. Several of the girls sit on them, adjusting their skates and talking to each other. Orly sits at the end of a bench and eyes me warily. "Give me a minute, Soph?"

"Sure, Orly." Janaye is already on the ice, and I skate over to her. "Been to the rink at Chelsea, Janaye?"

She grins at me, and I see that she's a little unsteady. "LeFrak, Soph, duh! In Prospect Park. But I've only been a couple of times!" I turn a circle around her and reach for her hand. She laughs. "Nuh uh, I'll fall on my butt!" I see only a couple of other girls out on the ice. Tess skates smoothly, in big arcs. That's not surprising, since she's from here. Chris is sitting on one of the benches by the bonfire on the shoreline. She doesn't have skates on. Keisha skates over to her and sits. They are too far away for me to hear them, but Chris shakes her head.

She's not far from Orly, and when I see Janaye sit, I skate in that direction. I don't want them hassling Orly. As I close in on them, I hear Chris explaining to Janaye that she never learned how to skate. Janaye offers to teach her, but Chris shakes her head. Yin skates up to them and sits with Chris also.

With both hands extended, I skate up to Orly farther down on the bench. "Are you ready to try?" She rolls her eyes, but smiles without opening her mouth and stands, holding on to the bench. "Take my hands and keep your knees bent, like when you can't reach anything to hang on to on the subway."

"Soph, slowly, please." She's still smiling, though. "I've never ridden the subway on skates!"

I can't help grinning. I do love the sound of skates on the ice, scraping and cutting. I watch Orly's eyes to make sure she doesn't panic and slowly skate backward, guiding her to the middle of the pond. "Orly, you're doing great!"

"I think you're doing it, Soph, not me." She's wobbly and hangs on to me hard.

I remember what my first instructor said. "Use your legs now to go forward; push a little with the edge of each skate when you do." She stumbles a little, but doesn't fall. Her face clouds, then eases. I encourage her. "Good! Take it slow." That makes me think of a children's song about a turtle my nanny used to play. I'm a terrible singer, but I try. "Take it from me. Sometimes you gotta take it slow!"

Orly laughs. "You're crazy, Soph. Good crazy, darlin', but crazy!" I let go of one of her hands, and her eyes widen. She stumbles, then rights herself, and I can see how graceful she is.

"I'm not going to let go of you altogether until you're ready; I promise!"

"Okay. I don't guess I get a free ride forever." She laughs shakily, and furrows her brow.

"Bend forward a little and tuck your arms in. Keep your body loose. You're doing super great!" I pivot, skate behind her, and come up next to her so that we're a pair. "Look at us!"

"Soph, you go on ahead. Show me what you can do."

I examine the open expanse of ice. It's usually much more crowded when I skate, except for lessons. I make a circle, then another one, then a figure eight. The cold air makes me feel as if I could go faster than ever before. I go to the far edge and look back at Orly, who has slowed to a stop and is looking at me expectantly. I build up speed and do a waltz jump. I hear whooping and look over to see several girls skating at one end of the pond. I can't help it. I bow my head and circle back to the far end. I know I'm showing off. I skate backward, holding Orly's gaze, gather speed, and then do a flip. My landing is shaky, but I hear more whoops and Orly grins, shaking her head.

I see Tess again. She's pretty good. She's not doing anything special, but she knows what she's doing and she's graceful. I wouldn't have put that together with what I know of her already: the funny combination of reserve and a steady indignation at everything I blurt out. She doesn't see me, so I turn and skate up next to her from behind. "Hi!"

"Very impressive, Soph."

I can't tell whether she's being honest or huffy. She has that type of voice. "Thanks! You must do a lot of skating yourself."

"Nothing fancy for me, Soph. But you know, up here the winter is long." She adds, "You're a really good skater. You look like a professional." I guess she was impressed after all.

Tess.

I ASSUMED SOPH DOESN'T KNOW how to skate, since she grew up in a city. I assumed wrong. Not only does she skate, not only did she bring her own expensive-looking skates, packed, apparently, by the same Betty who forgot her extra socks, but she's a figure skater, with fancy moves and that confidence she brings to everything. I find myself watching her do turns and flips. She looks beautiful on the ice, graceful and really happy to be there.

I'm a little worried about what Chris will do and, since I don't want to get involved, I stay on my own, watch Soph help Orly, and then do a couple of turns and a spin.

Someone has built a bonfire by the edge of the pond, and the staff brings out hot cider and doughnuts. We glide around in the cold for over an hour, showing each other what we know how to do on skates and laughing and falling. Chris has been sitting on the bench the whole time we've been out on the ice and I wonder why she won't even try. Orly is from the South too, but she has Soph pulling her around. I skate over to Chris and offer to help her find skates, but she just shakes her head at me.

"No, thanks, this seems pretty dangerous," she says and turns back to Yin, who is holding out her phone to share something.

I turn away and watch Soph doing a jump. She lands on one blade. When I turn back, Chris is standing by the fire talking to Janaye and Ellen and watching Orly. I'm not sure if Orly sees her or not. It makes me uncomfortable, so I make a point of going over to Orly and offering to skate with her while holding her hand.

We do that for a while. Her cheeks are pink from the cold, and she keeps saying, "My word, it's freezing," in a breathy Southern accent. I don't see any boy in her at all. Then I think I shouldn't be watching her like that, so I tell her about skating with my sister Molly when we were little and how I got mad because she was so much better than I was even though she was younger. Daddy told me to grow up, that I couldn't always expect to be the best at everything.

"Sisters, yes," she laughs. "My older one, Rose, she gets to do everything first. She gets the new clothes, the new shoes. I just get her hand-me-downs. She's a bossy know-it-all. When we were little she was always the queen and I was the servant. She still claims I was happy serving her all the time." We're both laughing, and Orly shakes her head at me, teasing. "So, I'm on Molly's side."

Soph catches our attention. She's doing an honest-to-god pirouette that has her turning backward midair and landing on one skate. You can hear everyone react.

Without warning, Orly falls. I stop help her up when, suddenly, Soph is right there next to her, holding out her hand. She asks Orly if she's hurt.

"No, I don't think so," Orly laughs. "But I daresay I've had enough ice for one day, thank you very much."

Soph and I each take one of her hands to help her skate back to the edge of the pond. The day is cold and sunny, and everything feels fresh.

Later, back in the room, changing for dinner, Soph carefully wipes the blades of her skates with a towel before she replaces the blade guards. I ask her about her skating.

Her hair is still mussed from pulling her hat off; her cheeks are bright from the cold. She folds the towel over again and shrugs. She tells me she isn't sure; her life got busy. "I still go once or twice a year, at Chelsea Piers," she says, snapping the second guard blade into place, "but my mother ruined it for me. She made it into a girly-princessy thing and I don't want to be her *infanta* in a *mantilla*, doing a triple axel for the social set." She frowns and then shakes her head, as if she can shake off whatever it is that her mother did. "I've never skated on a real pond before today. That was amazing."

"It was nice of you to teach Orly," I say without thinking and realize I've just opened up that conversation I told her I didn't want to have.

Soph looks at me hard. Then she says, "You know Chris is still at it." Her voice sounds different, wobbly but angry.

"I know," I say. "I offered to teach Chris how to skate, but she didn't want to."

Soph's expression is sharp. "Why would you even bother with her?"

I'm not quite sure what the answer to that is, so I try to explain. "I think it would be better if everyone could be friends. If Chris got to know Orly better, maybe she wouldn't be so scared of her."

"Orly's not scary," scoffs Soph.

I don't know what to say to that, because she's right.

✳   ✳   ✳

We are assigned to make dinner for that night, so, a half hour later, at about four-thirty, I pull on my shoes to go down to the kitchen. Dinner is supposed to be served at six-thirty. I'm doing calculations in my head about how long the meal will take to prepare and how to organize the cooking so everything is done at once. Soph is reading something on her phone. I stand by the door and wait for her to look up.

"Are you going somewhere?" She's still lounging on her stomach on the bed.

"Well, we have to make dinner tonight for everyone," I remind her. "We only have two hours, and I thought we should go down and get started."

She sits up then, phone dangling in her hand, and laughs that chirpy, cute laugh she has. "Oh, can't we just order Vietnamese or Middle Eastern dips and kebabs and let everyone choose what they want?"

I struggle to stop myself from rolling my eyes at her. *Different worlds, Tess*, I repeat in my head, *different worlds*.

"Soph, first of all, no, we're supposed to cook. They said they've got ingredients downstairs. And second, I don't have any money to pay for food for all these people."

She flinches and quickly says, "No, I didn't mean you would have to—I can put it on my card—" but I cut her off.

"Soph, you're in northern New Hampshire in the White Mountains. I've never even seen a Vietnamese restaurant, and there probably isn't a kebab anywhere around here either."

"You've never been to a Vietnamese restaurant? Seriously?" She is incredulous, eyes wide, staring at me like I come from Mars. This whole country mouse, city mouse routine is a little old, especially because *she* has come to *my* country. I decide to turn the tables on her.

"You mean *you've* never cooked dinner before?" And as soon as the words leave my mouth, she looks away and then at her lap while fiddling with her phone. I hit the nail on the head.

"C'mon," I say, reaching out to pull her up. "It's probably spaghetti and meatballs or something easy like that. I'll show you. It will be fun." She takes my hand then, briefly, and, for a split second, all I can think about is how warm it is in mine. I can feel my face turn red and I drop her hand as we walk downstairs without saying another word.

I'm almost right. The kitchen staff has laid out all the ingredients and a recipe for lasagna. We make two huge ones, regular and vegetarian, and, once we start, Soph is a good sport. She has no idea how to hold a knife, and I don't need to see any blood, so I cut onions and mushrooms. Soph stirs the sauce, which I tell her is important. Then I have her mix the cheese filling and lay the noodles in the pans.

"My MeMe, my grandmother, says you have to criss-cross the layers of noodles so it holds together better when you cut it," I tell her. Then I show her how to alternate the way the noodles stack with each layer. I stand close to her and see that her hands are a little messy from the cheese filling. When I notice her watching me intently, I back up fast. My cheeks warm again, and I turn back to the stove.

But she just asks me, "Does your MeMe live near you?"

"Yeah," I say, stirring the ground beef in the frying pan with much more attention than it deserves. "She lives in the same town. My grandfather died a few years ago, so we visit a lot to keep her company." I explain how we all go over to her house every week after church for Sunday dinner and how I always help her with the cooking.

"There's usually eleven of us, because my uncle comes with his family, so I'm used to cooking in big batches. I'm going to miss her when I leave next year."

"Wow!" Soph is watching me stir the sauce. "We almost never see my aunt and uncle. They live on the Main Line." I don't know where that is, but I assume it must be far from New York, or they would see each other more often. I turn the gas off.

We layer the two casseroles side by each. That's how we say "close to one another" where I'm from. Soph loves that expression. I tell her more about MeMe: how she still watches her soap opera on weekday afternoons and bakes cookies every Friday. Soph is practically giddy by the time the lasagnas are ready to go in the oven.

"No, wait!" she says, as I open the big commercial oven to put them in, "I need to take a picture! No one at home will believe I made this myself!"

She didn't make it *herself*, but I smile patiently, and put the pans back on the counter while she pulls out her phone.

"You too," she says, and pulls me in close for a selfie with her and one of the big pans of lasagna. I do the classic selfie pose, opening my mouth and raising my eyebrows as if I am surprised to be having my picture taken. She laughs when she shows me the shot. She has a smudge of tomato sauce on her cheek, and my hair is coming out of its ponytail, so it's messy on one side.

"Sweet," she says, and then holds the oven door open for me while I slide the two pans in. Then I show her how to make salad and garlic bread. At the end, I teach her to let the lasagna sit for ten minutes before cutting it so the whole dish will come together before we cut into it.

After we put the food out on the serving tables, I turn to find a seat toward the end of the table. I expect Soph will go back to the middle where she sat with Janaye, but she surprises me by plopping down next to me instead. When Orly comes in, Soph waves her over, and Orly sits down across from us with a small sigh. Soph tells her excitedly about making dinner.

Orly says she cooks with her grandmother. She tells us a funny story about how, when she was little, she used to think black-eyed peas really had eyes and she was terrified they were watching her eat them. I tease Soph a little about wanting to come to Minerva for four years without so much as knowing they don't have ethnic restaurants around. It all feels comfortable and friendly, until I see Chris taking notes on the other side of the table.

* * *

From Soph Alcazar's Writing Journal,
February 13, 2018

What I do well, I am able to teach,
But she shows me something new, side by each.

Chapter Fourteen

From the Fan Fiction Unbound Archive,
posted by conTessaofthecastle:

The next morning, Daphne awoke with a start, looking for Astoria. No one was there. Daphne wasn't sure how the magic had changed, but she knew she would only be able to figure it out if she found Astoria again. Sighing, she packed up the blanket and the single bowl they had been using for meals. She made sure the campfire was completely doused, strewed the ashes and covered them with leaves. If the Coven came this way they would probably be able to sense her presence, but she didn't want to give them any obvious clues. The sun was out today at least, and Daphne checked its position as she murmured the pathfinder chant to make sure she was headed east, toward the Portal of Arden. She didn't know what else to do.

Soph.

WEDNESDAY MORNING WHEN I WAKE UP, I find, to my surprise, that Freddy has texted me. It's Valentine's Day, but that's not the point of Freddy's text.

[FROM FREDDY TO SOPH] *Help! They're insisting I ski this time.*

I suppose it was bound to happen. Mrs. Peckett can be very persuasive.

[FROM SOPH TO FREDDY] *Just do the bunny trail once then say you twisted your ankle.*

[FROM FREDDY TO SOPH] *It's been three years. Last time I fell it was a total yard sale. I broke my collarbone.*

[FROM SOPH TO FREDDY] *You can fall on the bunny slope—everyone else there does.*

[FROM FREDDY TO SOPH] *But ski instructor is 2 hot. He'll laugh at me.*

Well, that answers the question: Freddy's gay, like me, or maybe bi or pan. Did he think I already knew?

[FROM SOPH TO FREDDY] *Gotta pretend to try. Then be damsel in distress!*

Freddy responds with an emoji of a princess. He turns out to have more personality than I thought.

[FROM SOPH TO FREDDY] *Good to try new things.*

I attach the selfie of Tess and me holding the lasagna.

[From Freddy to Soph] *Since when is lasagna a new thing?*

[FROM SOPH TO FREDDY] *No, we made the lasagna. Ourselves!*

[FROM FREDDY TO SOPH] *Cool. And the girl in the picture?*

This time, he puts in a winking emoji.

[FROM SOPH TO FREDDY] *Room8. Nice girl. Different tribe.*

He turns serious.

[FROM FREDDY TO SOPH] *Don't tell anyone.*

[FROM SOPH TO FREDDY] *OK.*

But I can't help adding,

[FROM SOPH TO FREDDY] *UR late to the party, F. Time to come out!*

[FROM FREDDY TO SOPH] *UR the only one I told. Please.*

[FROM SOPH TO FREDDY] *Why did you wait so long?*

[From Freddy to Soph] *Too hard.*

[From Soph to Freddy] *Duh. But it only gets harder.*

[From Freddy to Soph] *There's no other way?*

[From Soph to Freddy] *NO!!!*

[From Freddy to Soph] *Know it all.*

Tess hears me say "humph" out loud.

"Did you say something, Soph?"

"No, I'm getting frustrated with this guy."

"A guy?"

"Yeah, well, no, not that. I know this guy, Freddy, and he just told me that he's gay but he won't tell his parents or anyone. I wish he would come out already."

"Why do you care?"

"Because he's going to have to at some point. You have to come out if you want to live your life. I did it. My queer friends did it too. Freddy's parents will find out sooner or later. He should tell them now. It feels a lot better after you do."

Tess seems to ponder this. She probably doesn't understand. Straight people don't.

"You sound pretty certain about that."

"It's a fact, Tess. Coming out is better for everyone. We can't hide in the closet forever, you know." I'm getting worked up over this and I probably shouldn't. If Tess is from a military family, she probably isn't too keen on gays. I don't think they even had Don't Ask Don't Tell when her father went to Iraq. That's over now, but I bet things haven't changed that much. Now she's frowning at me.

"Maybe he will someday, Soph. Why does it have to be right away?"

"Because there are other gay kids, and the more of us who are out, the less we can be oppressed. We need to build our own community." Tess picks up her phone and starts texting, probably to the boyfriend again.

After a minute she says quietly, "But he did come out, didn't he?" I look at her.

"He came out to you. Isn't that enough, if it's enough for him?"

Like I said, straight people don't get it. I pick up my phone again, thinking I'll text Gordon, Mibs, and Lally. Except I promised Freddy I wouldn't tell. I realize Tess is right. He did come out to me. It's a start.

❋   ❋   ❋

I'M A LITTLE NERVOUS GOING into the second group session on Wednesday morning. I'm glad that we decided to do a ballad, but so many of these girls aren't what I expected. Yin seems fine when we talk, but she was hanging out with Chris and piling on Orly. I wish she'd get over that. I had a good time making dinner with Tess. Sometimes it seems she likes me, like when we were skating or when she was teasing me about going to college in New Hampshire, but we're really different. I hope I can avoid Professor Forsythe, at least until I figure out how to make a better impression.

We meet in one of the third-floor rooms, but no one is focused, so I start. "We're doing a ballad. What kind of story do we want to tell?"

"Obviously, it should be about a woman," Ellen offers to general assent.

"Should we do a love story? Maybe a tragic one? For Valentine's?" It makes sense to me that Gabriela would propose this. She's got a tragic streak and a boyfriend.

Yin wants us to do something which has a compelling story, including a journey and something our protagonist learns after overcoming a great challenge.

I'm fine with this, but it doesn't help us narrow anything down. "Do we want to make up characters?"

"No way. Too much work. Ballads like Beowulf are from oral history. Let's work with a story which is already out there." Ellen's right.

We can't decide between comic book heroines and historical feminists until Gabriela suggests we try a goddess from one of the Greek myths. "We could do Demeter and Persephone. I love that story! Demeter helps her daughter Persephone escape from Hades, but Persephone has to return six months a year because she ate six pomegranate seeds while she was there. Demeter is the goddess of the harvest and is depressed when her daughter is away, which turns the season dark and cold."

"But there's no lesson to that one. It explains winter, that's all," Yin complains.

I ask if anyone knows any other Greek or Roman goddesses, maybe in nontraditional relationships. The general answer is that they're all married with god-kids.

"Why are we doing Greek or Roman goddesses. What about a Norse one?"

"Does anyone know any Norse gods?" Gabriela asks.

"I do," Ellen volunteers. "My mom's family is from Sweden. I grew up hearing about them."

We settle on Freya. Ellen says she's the chief goddess. We use our phones to do some quick research on her. She's the goddess of love, sex, beauty, fertility, gold, war, and death—try to beat that. She's married to another god, Od, and has a chariot pulled by two cats. Freya has a magic necklace of desire that makes her irresistible to men and a cloak made of falcon feathers that allows her to turn into a bird and fly.

"It says there are already epic poems about her, including an appearance in Beowulf."

"Why don't we change her?" I suggest, thinking I want her to be bisexual and definitely have a wife.

Yin goes along with it. "Great idea—enough with the same old binary stuff!"

I wonder if she realizes this is basically fan fiction. For once, I decide to keep my mouth shut.

Tess.

CHRIS DOESN'T BOTHER TO COME to this morning's group meeting. I don't know where she is. Part of me thinks she might be upstairs going through Orly's things, which gives me a slightly sick feeling in my stomach, but I decided not to involve myself and I'm going to stick to that decision unless something changes.

Peggy, Keisha, and I are brainstorming plot points, and then Peggy drafts a description of the town. I use my phone to research Maizy Donovan's character. We decided to stick with the original idea, because I keep hoping I can figure out a way to convince Chris to work with us and because, after finding some background online about Ultraman comics, I'm pretty excited about Maizy's character.

Ultraman started in the 1970s, and Maizy is described as a "bold and fearless career woman, seeking out the truth wherever it may take her." Not surprisingly, the truth leads her straight to Ultraman over and over, but I like that Maizy is ahead of her time. Ultraman keeps flirting with her, and she keeps him at arm's length until she solves the mystery for her newspaper article. She might let him kiss her now and then or fly her out of danger, but she's not all clingy and needy. In fact, until the comic gets sold to a new publisher in 1985, she's very independent. After 1985, she wears tight clothes and screams to be rescued from bad guys in almost every panel. The comic got cancelled in 1993, right after Maizy and Ultraman got married.

We agree to go back to the early days. I research some big news stories from that time. I have a hard time understanding that this was how the world was when my mom and dad were born. I decide to write about Maizy's fight to be paid the same amount as the dashing investigative journalist Ron Reynolds. From what I'm reading, lots of women were joining the workforce in the 1970s but didn't have the legal protections they do now. Men weren't fired for "sexual harassment," nor did women always understand they were entitled to equal pay for equal work. I think that at least sounds like something Chris would be interested in following up on, if she ever shows up. Even if she doesn't, I think it will make a good story.

Peggy, Keisha, and I work pretty efficiently, and it's much easier without Chris. Keisha is funny and smart and she takes notes on her laptop since I don't have one. She offers to let me use it after

lunch so I can draft some parts more easily. I'm a little uneasy
about that, because she says she's going to hang out with Chris
while I use it, but I decide to try to be friends.

At noon Joan ends the session, and we go to lunch. When I sit
at the table next to Keisha, I find that Chris is there already, talking
to Clover and Janaye in low tones about why Orly shouldn't be
here. Clover beckons me, but I look away. I really don't want to
do this. When Soph comes in with Orly, Chris and Janaye stop
talking. I'm liking this less and less, and now I think I should say
something to someone. None of the adults have arrived when
Soph looks out the window of the dining room as she's pulling
out her chair and asks in a loud voice, "What the actual fuck?"

We all turn to see what she's pointing at. Our snowsisters from
the other night are lined up outside. They're a little ragged, since
it kept snowing, and most of them have snowdrifts clinging to
them. But I see it immediately. Someone took the carrot nose
from the snowsister Soph and Orly built, with its lacy black bra,
and shoved it down lower. To make a penis.

✳　✳　✳

From Soph Alcazar's Writing Journal,
February 14, 2018

Come out, join the group, acknowledge yourself.
Those who persecute us can go to hell.

Chapter Fifteen

From the Fan Fiction Unbound Archive,
posted by conTessaofthecastle:

Daphne hid behind a tree as the carriage passed by. Much as she wanted to wave down the driver and ask for a ride, it was too risky. She closed her eyes and tried reciting the shape-shifting spell again. Nothing happened, except that the sound of carriage wheels stopped.

"Who's there?" called a voice. A horse shook its bridle.

Daphne froze.

Soph.

I CAN'T BELIEVE IT. SOMEONE put a dick on our snowsister. I have no doubt it was Chris. I'm still in socks or I'd go out there, grab it, and stick it right in Chris's face. But before I can say anything beyond my initial outburst, I see Tess come around the corner outside the window. She trudges through the fresh snow over to our snowsister and grabs the carrot. Then she trudges back around the corner. A minute later, she's inside, and everyone is frozen in their places. She doesn't close the door all the way behind her.

"I don't know who did this," she says, looking in the direction of Chris, Keisha, and Yin. Tess doesn't yell, but her voice is clear and firm. I'm surprised and impressed. I realize that she has an accent, but not the New England accent you hear on television. Hers is softer, and it gives her steady voice force. "But if people have something to say, they should say it. And if they aren't going to say it, they should keep it to themselves."

Chris lifts her chin at Tess. "Who are you to judge, Tess?" She doesn't say she was the one who did it. But she doesn't deny it either.

Tess stares her down; her blue-green eyes are very hard. "I'm not judging. I'm saying if anyone is *going* to judge, they should do so openly so everyone who is judged can respond. And everyone else can see what's going on." Wow! I didn't expect this from Tess. She keeps talking. "You know, I've tried to be friends with everyone here. And I tried to stay out of it. But this isn't okay anymore. This is just—" She searches for the right word and then finds it. "Mean. Just plain mean."

When did Tess start to talk like this? For the last two nights, she hasn't wanted to get involved. She could barely defend her own writing, the first day.

I'm nervous about how Orly will react, but she rolls her eyes and says in a calm voice, "Well, bless your heart, isn't that a tall drink of iced tea, Chris?" A few of the girls titter.

Chris looks back at Orly with her eyes narrowed. She turns on her heel and walks out of the room. Not even Keisha and Yin follow her.

After Chris leaves, Orly says, "I generally expect at least eighteen karats on Valentine's Day, maybe twenty-four."

Lunch is very quiet.

* * *

WHEN I GO BACK UPSTAIRS to get my laptop charger, Chris is coming out of her room with a duffel bag. I don't see Orly.

"Are you leaving?" I ask her. That might be for the best.

"Moving up to one of the third-floor rooms," she says, her voice clipped. "I don't need y'all hassling me anymore. I'm here to write."

"Did you do it?" She ignores me and strides down the hall toward the third-floor stairs.

I find Orly in a corner of the lounge, reading off her phone. "Are you all right, Orly?"

"I suppose I'm fine," she responds. "This is nothing new. But I appreciate that Tess called them out."

I want to say something like "I support you," but I realize that sounds pretty patronizing. Instead I say, "I wanted to know if you have any extra socks I could borrow. Tess loaned me these, but I don't want to keep them all week, and I forgot to pack extras."

Orly shakes her head. "Sorry, hon. I don't own many pairs myself and I didn't bring any extras. Y'all have some cold weather up here!"

As I'm about to leave, Orly asks me not to say anything to the instructors. "Chris is gone," she says. "I don't want everyone here to think I'm a problem."

I try to tell her she's not the problem, but she seems pretty convinced. "Soph, it was pretty clear from the beginning that me-'n-her weren't gonna mix. I've got no need to keep this on everyone's plate."

Rather than argue, I tell her I'll keep quiet. On my way back to our room, I think about the fact that Tess confronted Chris about the carrot, but Orly referred to "everyone here." We have time, so I take out my phone.

[FROM SOPH TO GORDON, LALLY, AND MIBS] *UR not going to believe this.*

[FROM MIBS TO GORDON, LALLY, AND SOPH] *Wut?*

[FROM SOPH TO GORDON, LALLY, AND MIBS] *Jerk put a dick on our snowsister.*

[FROM GORDON TO LALLY, MIBS, AND SOPH] *Who's your snowsister?*

He adds a winky emoticon.

[FROM SOPH TO GORDON, LALLY, AND MIBS] *Snowman, but a woman. Mean girl made carrot nose a dick.*

[FROM MIBS TO GORDON, LALLY, AND SOPH] *More transphobes. What do they care?*

[FROM SOPH TO GORDON, LALLY, AND MIBS] *Right. Then room8 got salty af!*

[FROM GORDON TO LALLY, MIBS, AND SOPH] *Military room8 with BF?*

[FROM SOPH TO GORDON, LALLY, AND MIBS] *Yup.*

[FROM GORDON TO LALLY, MIBS, AND SOPH] *She sounds cool.*

✳ ✳ ✳

IN THE AFTERNOON, WE ARE supposed to have a check-in meeting with our instructors about our individual work. I sign up to meet with Grace later in the afternoon. I'm working on a sonnet about how this week is going. It's not in couplets, but still the simple Shakespearean style.

> *Here I came, my purpose only to learn.*
> *I quickly found the perfect one to teach*
> *Me. Instead her scorn is all I can earn,*
> *Though her attention I try and beseech.*

> *Meanwhile, my peers I don't understand.*
> *One of us they have needlessly maligned.*
> *We should be enlightened, offer our hands,*
> *All of us writers, interests aligned.*

> *Disharmony under the surface lurks,*
> *Divided, scattered, and not together*
> *On subjects much less worthy than our works.*
> *Progress impossible, oeuvres no better.*

> *I'm stuck in gloom, all my spirits weighted,*
> *My objectives all being frustrated.*

I give this to Grace when I see her. I know the poem is not great. But it does reflect how I feel, and I don't have much else to show her. She sighs when she finishes.

"Soph, are you having that bad a time? I heard you were a star at skating and plenty of the other girls want to hang out with you."

Now I feel like a whiny brat. But Grace is only talking about the stupid social stuff, and it's not as if I met a girlfriend or anything. I change the conversation to my writing. If Yin is right, I might be able to use Grace as a reference for Minerva. The admissions office would probably be impressed with that.

"I'm fine. I feel as if my work isn't going anywhere. I expected something different from this week."

Grace adopts a frank tone. "Soph, you want to write according to specific structures, right? You already know how to make a template with a spreadsheet. The hard part, and one you can work on, is capturing emotion and using words with feeling. Poetry is not only saying something in a patterned way, but pulling the words together so that their sound and their meaning contribute to the verse."

I nod, even though I'm still skeptical.

"Let's go over a few of your lines. The second to last one, 'I'm stuck in gloom, all my spirits weighted,' is exactly what I'm talking about. That line is dark and heavy, not only the meaning of the words, but their sounds and shapes as well. 'Weighted' and 'gloom' and 'stuck.' The other words in this line don't interfere, they let the meaningful ones stand out."

We go through some other lines, and I'm surprised that she is so good at analyzing the strengths and weaknesses in my work. Maybe she *is* a decent instructor for me.

Tess.

LATE IN THE AFTERNOON, AFTER a really quiet individual writing session, Soph and I go up to our room.

On the stairs she says, "Hey, Tess, that was nice of you, sticking up for Orly. How come you decided to do that?"

Before I think about it I say, "Because Chris crossed a line. And Joey would have wanted me to do something about it."

She starts a little when I say that and asks, "Why would your boyfriend care?"

I realize I've said too much and just shake my head at her. Before she can press the issue, we reach our room, where a box addressed to Soph is sitting on the floor outside the door. The logo on it is L.L.Bean. She must have ordered herself a brand-new pair of snow boots and had them shipped overnight. I still do not understand the world Soph lives in.

"What?" She shrugs as we go inside. She plops down on the bed, pulls the boots out of the box, and works on the laces. I smile, not wanting to disturb the truce we forged when I stood up for Orly. I know why I did it, even if I'm not ready to talk about it here with these girls.

I change the subject. "I talked to Yin and Keisha. They said they didn't do it. Yin was willing to go talk to Professor Forsythe with Chris, but now she doesn't want any part of Chris. They both said this went too far. So, I'm pretty sure Chris did it."

Soph looks impressed.

I wish I could talk to Joey. Even though I know that he would tell me to talk about it, sometimes it helps to hear him say it out loud.

Soph's phone goes off with an incoming text, and she groans.

"Your mom again?" I ask, since that's how she reacts to all of her mom's texts.

"Yes," she says, annoyed. "Listen to this." She reads, in a high-pitched voice. "'S—what about upswept hair? You used to love when we did that with the Castilian comb.'"

"What's she talking about?" I ask.

Soph flings herself on her bed dramatically. "That stupid debutante ball again," she says. "She's actually planning how I'm going to wear my hair a whole year ahead of time!"

"It sounds really formal and fancy, like a wedding," I say. "What's the what's-it-called comb?"

"It's a Spanish thing. You start with this ornate metal comb called a *pieneta* and then you overlay it with a scarf, which goes down the back of your head. That part is the *mantilla*."

I like the way she says the Spanish words with an accent. Her t's are softer, and the vowels roll. She shows me pictures of the Spanish royal family on her phone.

"See how Queen Sofia wears it? My mom loves that because she's not Spanish herself, the same way Queen Sofia isn't, but everyone appreciates how she wears the *pieneta y mantilla* for special occasions. Here is Sofia at her wedding before she was the Queen. My parents called me Sophronia partly because of her. She was Princess of Greece and Denmark before she married Juan Carlos."

"Wow! It looks like you'd have to practice to keep it from falling off your head."

"You do," she says sullenly.

I want to ask if she knows any of the queens or princesses in the photos, but her tone stops me. "Don't you like Queen Sofia too?"

"I don't know. She's not too big on the gay community. She's against gay marriage, because she's Catholic. She has a right to her opinion. But she has hurt a lot of feelings. Maybe the new

Queen, Letizia, will be better." She pronounces it *Lay-teeth-ee-a*. She shrugs.

Soph's indifference surprises me. If Queen Sofia is anti-gay, I'd expect Soph to take a stronger stand. Instead of asking her more I say, "I think you'd look nice in it, the… *pieneta*." I try to say it right but it comes out like *piñata*. "The comb would stand out against your hair."

"I did used to love playing dress-up with that comb when I was little," she says, and a smile plays on her face. "My grandmother Alicia gave it to my mom for her wedding." *A-leeth-ee-a*. I love how she says the names. "I think it was made specially for *her* mother at the end of the 1800s."

The smile fades quickly, though, and she says, "But it still feels wrong to me. I mean, I don't want to be dressed up like a pretty little doll on the arm of some guy I don't know or care about, so that I can see my picture in a social-set story."

I laugh, and Soph pouts. "No, I'm not laughing at you. I guess I have a hard time thinking of you as anybody's pretty little doll." She smirks at that. "Don't you know some boy who is a friend you could ask? If you went with someone you know, it might turn out to be more fun than you think. And you'd make your mom happy at the same time."

"I don't know," she sighs. "I think Mrs. Peckett, the one who gave me a ride up here, wants me to ask her son Freddy."

"So why not do that?" I ask.

"He's not…" She stops.

"What?" Now I'm curious.

"He's not the person I want to dress up for like that," she finally says, "but I guess I could think about it."

✳ ✳ ✳

From Soph Alcazar's Writing Journal,
February 14, 2018

Friends from afar are the ones who get me.
I try not to let these girls upset me.

Chapter Sixteen

From the Fan Fiction Unbound Archive,
posted by conTessaofthecastle:

Daphne knew she couldn't stay hidden. Whoever was in that carriage must have magical powers also, to have felt her presence. She recalled the words her mother spoke, the night before Astoria and Daphne left the Coven, "When a witch acts, she must do so deliberately or not at all. Magical intent must be chosen, not stumbled upon, or its effect will be disastrous."

Soph.

AT DINNER, PROFESSOR FORSYTHE ANNOUNCES that Grace will read her poetry in the lounge later, and everyone is invited to attend, but it isn't mandatory. Grace tells one of the other girls that Professor Forsythe, Joan, and Celestine are planning to take the evening off and go into town, which explains why the three of them disappear before dessert.

Before we leave the table, Grace stands up. "Even though I'm reading from my own recent material tonight, I thought we'd put on an impromptu poetry slam first. Let's be very casual about it. You don't have to prepare anything. Instead, plan to just say something if the mood strikes you. It can be serious or silly, topical or not. Let's all put on pajamas and sweats and have fun with it."

As we clear our places, I hear rain outside, something I didn't expect since it has been so cold. Climbing the stairs, I ask Tess if that means winter is letting up already.

"I don't think so, Soph. Joey texted that a surprise ice storm just passed through there. He's stuck at home." Her face clouds over before she changes the subject. "Those teachers shouldn't be out in this. Listen to that wind."

Back in our room, the tip of a tree branch brushes against the window as it whips around. It's too dark to see outside. Tess remarks, "That means the roads will be bad. It rains, then it freezes. Everything will be covered with ice."

I change into yoga pants, noticing that Tess keeps her jeans on, rather than putting on pink sweats or her camouflage pajama bottoms. We go back down to the lounge with everyone else, taking seats on one of the couches which line three sides of the room. I guess no one decided to stay in their room.

Grace stands up at the front in a sweatshirt and plaid pajama bottoms. "I'm sure some of us know what a poetry slam is, but for those who don't, it's a performance competition. People get up and deliver poems about whatever subjects matter to them. Usually the audience judges which are the best, but I thought we'd try something different. We won't bother with winners or losers. However, each girl's poem should be linked somehow to the poem that went before it. If you have a different topic, think about how you can connect it to the girl who's just gone. This is from a Persian practice called *mushaira*. Let's try it."

At first, no one volunteers. We stare at each other until Orly puts a hand up. "May I go first, Grace?"

Orly stands. She looks around at the group.

"With best intentions, kindly or not, you all empathize
with my dilemma.
Only you don't.

"You think you know I'm between two worlds, male and
female, inside and out.
But I'm not.

"I'm a girl. I'm not caught between being a boy or a girl.
I'm a girl. I'm not halfway or in transition or lost.
I'm a girl.

"You've seen me insulted and you think I'm hurt.
Darlings, you've no idea.

"I'm a girl. I'm not wounded by a carrot.
I'm a girl. I'm not defined by anyone else.
I'm a girl.

"Let me tell you my dilemma.
How do I approach this world?

"I'm a girl. That's all I should have to say.
I'm a girl. That should be enough.
Maybe I shouldn't even have to say that.

"But I've been through more than your average girl.
I'm a trans girl. I'm proud that I've made it to where I am.
I want to be recognized.

I want you to validate my triumph over a cruel biological fluke.
I want you to know that I had to strive to be fully me.
I want you to understand: That's okay.
I want you to think, "She did it. She's beautiful."

"I'm a girl *and* I'm a trans girl.
Do I need to say I'm both?
Can I just show up?"

No one speaks when Orly sits down, but a few girls are making jazz hands. I can't hear anyone breathing.

I'm surprised when Yin gets up next. I was just about to, but she beat me to it. Her voice is clear.

"I was wrong.
I played along.
But you're above the fray,
And what you say,
That's the way
We should get along.

"You can just show up.
It is beautiful.
You are beautiful.
No one can tell you what you are.
You've defined yourself in ways most of us never will.
I can say back to you, 'You're a girl. You're a trans girl.'
I don't have your answer.

But if there is an answer, I believe you'll find it.

If you just show up, I'll just show up with you."

Out of the corner of my eye, I spot Chris. She darts out of the room toward the stairs. No one else seems to notice.

Tess.

WHEN YIN FINISHES, EVERYONE SNAPS their fingers or makes jazz hands. Soph stands up to take a turn when, suddenly, the lights go out, plunging the room into darkness. The snapping stops, and I hear Keisha say, "Hey!"

"Would you turn the lights back on, please?" It's Grace. "Come on, very funny."

The wind howls, and the rain beats on the windows. I tell Grace, "I think the power's out. It happens in ice storms. The cables break in the wind or pull away from the telephone poles. Who's got their phones?"

A few lights go on around the room. I can't make out any faces, just bright little spotlights. "We don't all need to use them at once. We should conserve the batteries in case the lights don't come back for a while."

Grace gets up, "I'm going to find candles, and then we'll continue. Everyone stay put, please."

"This is like a horror movie," Peggy says. "The grown-ups leave and the next thing you know, we hear the killer upstairs."

As if on cue, a loud thump and the sound of breaking glass come from upstairs. The building shakes. A couple of girls yelp.

I say, "It sounds as if a tree fell, maybe that one outside our room. It could have broken our window."

Someone asks, "Where's Chris?"

"I saw her leave after Yin's poem."

"Do you think that was her upstairs?"

I am sick of Chris, but we should make sure she's okay. "Can someone text her or call her to see where she is?" No one speaks up.

That's when we figure out that no one has her cell number.

"Why would we, Tess? She's been awful." Keisha says. "She wouldn't even work on our group project."

"Because, Keisha, she could be hurt or frightened. She's part of our group. I should have gotten her number. Whether anyone likes her or not, you don't leave a soldier on the field."

"Chris as a fallen soldier—I'm not touching that one," Orly jokes. The others murmur assent. I guess I shouldn't be surprised. Chris is mad at both Soph and me. I thought she was still friends with Janaye and Clover. She had some supporters, at least at the beginning of the week. But everyone's reaction to Orly's poetry must have felt like a slap in the face. Orly continues, "We all heard glass breaking. She could be hurt."

"I'll go. She's right next to our room," I offer. "I want to see if our window broke anyway."

"No, she moved up to the third floor. I saw her," It's Soph.

"Then I'll go up there. I still want to see if our window's broken."

Soph volunteers, "I'll go with Tess. Anyone else for follow-the-leader?

No one else speaks, so I stand and put my cell phone light on. Soph takes my hand as we walk back to the stairs. That startles me.

"Peggy said it's a horror movie. I can't watch those alone." She squeezes my hand. It feels nice.

We climb the stairs to the third floor. All the doors are open except one. I drop Soph's hand to knock. There's no answer. I point my cell phone at myself and raise my eyebrows in a silent question.

Soph whispers, "Well, she doesn't like me. *You* ask."

I knock again. "Chris? It's Tess. Are you okay? Everyone else is downstairs."

We hear her inside. "Go away. I'm fine. I'm not going back downstairs." Her voice is thin, as though she hurt herself or is frightened.

"Chris," Soph asks, "are you sure you're okay? You don't sound fine. And we heard a crash downstairs."

Chris coughs, then speaks to us through the door, "I think that tree outside fell over. Just leave me alone." She sounds a little better this time, but not much.

"Chris, please come to the door. Let us see that you're safe, and we'll leave you alone." I try to sound as if I know what I'm doing.

Chris is quiet for a minute or two, then the door cracks open inward. Chris squints at the light from my phone. The wind howls behind her, much louder than it should be from inside a building. Her face is blotchy; she's been crying.

"What are you doing here?" she asks.

* * *

From Soph Alcazar's Writing Journal,
February 14, 2018

The slam poem enlightens us, so true.
The villain alights, into black, not blue.

Chapter Seventeen

From the Fan Fiction Unbound Archive,
posted by conTessaofthecastle:

Taking a breath, Daphne stepped from behind the tree.

Soph.

CHRIS HAS A PARKA ON, as though she's headed outside. Cold air blows on my face from the doorway. "Chris, do you have your window open? I can feel the wind."

Chris's eyes widen. She takes a long breath, and opens her door wider. Her window is broken, and it's even colder inside her room than in the hall. The wind blows in ice and rain. "The tree branch hit the window about ten minutes ago."

"Chris, you can't stay in there. At least come to our room downstairs."

She shakes her head. "I'm fine. I have a jacket on. I moved the furniture away from the window so it wouldn't get wet. I can go to a room down the hall."

She continues, "I'm not going downstairs to be poetry-slammed. Now go away."

Tess takes a different tack. "Chris, no one is going to slam you. Let's talk about it. Everyone is downstairs. The power went out. We noticed you were missing and came to find you because we were worried." She doesn't mention that no one has Chris's number.

"I doubt that." Chris snorts. "Can you leave me alone, please?"

Tess looks at me, and I look back at her. I think neither of us is sure what to do. Tess reaches out and grabs Chris by the arm.

"If you don't want to go down to the lounge, fine. But we aren't leaving you here. Come sit in our room where at least it's warmer."

Chris starts to pull her arm back, but Tess's grip must be firm, because she doesn't let go.

Chris sighs, "Hang on, let me get my phone."

I'm surprised Tess convinced her, but I was also surprised Tess wanted to try. Tess has been surprising me all week.

Tess follows Chris into the room. I can make out Chris fumbling for her phone in the dark. Tess turns on her flashlight to help, then pulls a blanket off the bed. She drops it quickly. "Chris, this is soaking wet!"

A few minutes later, we are on the second floor in our room. It's dark and colder than before, but not nearly as loud or as cold as it was in Chris's room. Tess shuts our door and turns off her flashlight. The three of us stand there uncertainly.

"I bet you're colder than you're letting on, Chris. This isn't Texas, and you're all damp."

Tess rummages through her duffel, and I reach into mine. We turn back to Chris at the same time. She lights up her phone to see what we're offering. Tess holds up her pink camo pajamas, and I have Papa's unopened bottle of Hennessy. Chris's teeth chatter in the dark. She looks at both of us, unsure what to reach for first.

*   *   *

I never would have expected to find Chris wearing Tess's pajamas and sitting in my bed with the two of us. But there we are. Tess texts Keisha to tell her that we're fine, but we're not going back down and the lodge should arrange for Chris's window to be boarded up. She convinces Chris to change into her pajamas and explains that the three of us should huddle together for warmth.

"What are you, some kind of Girl Scout?" Chris asks.

"Yes," Tess answers firmly. She's a lot more confident than when we arrived last weekend. "Gold Award. And I do a lot of hunting with my dad in the winter, and, you know, I happened to grow up here. Consider it a tip from the locals."

"I'll drink to that!" I announce, holding the bottle high. That's when the three of us climb into my bed and pull the comforters from both beds over us. I get in first, on the left, followed by Tess. Chris sits on Tess's other side. I take a big pull of the Hennessy and try to explain how Lally, Gordon, Mibs, and I hang out on the steps of the Met at night.

"I don't get it, Soph. You and your friends go to a museum for fun?"

"No, Tess. We just hang out on the steps. The Met's closed by the time we get there. Kids from all the schools go and sit there at night. We just chill."

Chris doesn't say anything. I pass the bottle to Tess. I sit right up against her. I like the way her leg feels next to mine. I'm glad it's dark in here.

Tess takes a tiny sip. "This stuff burns!"

I snort. "Keep going, you'll get used to it. Can't you feel it make you warmer?"

Tess shrugs, right next to my shoulder. "I guess so. My fingers feel less numb."

We pass the bottle around, and I tease Tess a little. "I can't believe a Gold Star Girl Scout and West Point wannabe is risking it all tonight, Tess. Is this your first time getting drunk?"

Tess laughs in a relaxed way I haven't heard before, like she's less controlled. She takes the bottle and this time she really drinks from it, not just a little sip, but a gulp. "Nope. We have parties in Castleton. But usually beer or vodka people sneak out in water bottles from their dads' liquor cabinets." She tells a story about a girl whose parents came home early and caught everyone drinking.

"Do you get drunk with Joey?" I can see Chris pause with the bottle when I ask.

Tess twitches next to me. "Why would I do that?"

"I thought guys like to get their girlfriends drunk before making out."

Chris speaks for what seems like the first time. "Sounds pervy!" Leaning over Tess, she hands the bottle to me. "Maybe she should tell us more about her and this guy. I noticed she didn't say no."

Tess.

I MAY BE FEELING WARMER and a little better about Chris, but I am *not* sharing private details about what I do with Joey. "'S off limits." I realize I'm starting to slur my words. Oh, brother!

Soph hands the bottle back to me. "You almost never want to talk about him. Didn't he send you a Valentine?"

I take another sip. I know I have to change the subject.

"Not talking about Joey. Do you have a girlfriend, Soph?" Although my mind is fuzzier from the alcohol, I realize I don't know the answer to this question even though we've been living in one room for almost a week now.

"Tragically, no," she says. "The only two other out girls at my school are dating each other. And neither of them is really my type anyway."

The alcohol must be doing its job, because this is stuff I never talk about with anyone, not even Joey. I really want to ask how a girl figures out what kind of girl she likes. The bottle is already heading back my way, so I take it and turn toward Chris to ask if she's dating anyone. I'm just trying to be polite—and change the subject.

"I was. For two years. He went to Baylor last fall and broke up with me by text." Her answer surprises me. Chris seems so independent, as if she doesn't need anyone. The idea of her with a boy for that long, an older boy who went to college, is hard to wrap my head around.

I'm still figuring out what to say as I take another sip from the bottle, but before I do, Soph says, "Asshole," which sounds appropriate.

"He wasn't, though, Soph." This is the first time tonight Chris has used either of our names. Her voice, slightly slurred like mine, sounds sad. "He was brilliant and nice. Cute, too, with brown curly hair." Her voice cracks. "Romantic, even. He read Beat poetry to me and played music on old vinyl records." She stops before resuming, "I don't know why he dumped me and I don't guess I'll ever find out."

"'S that why you always want to investigate things? So, you can figure it out and win him back?" I ask without thinking. Chris has the bottle. She takes a sip before answering me.

"No. Don't be stupid, Tess." I guess we aren't going to be besties by the end of the night after all. She goes on. "I like knowing why things happen, uncovering what the inside story is. I hate guessing about things. I want to have facts. He texted once and told me it was over and then never again. I have all these questions and I—I guess I wanted to know what I did wrong, so I don't do it again with my next boyfriend."

I think she's going to hand the bottle to Soph, but she rests it on her lap and peers sideways at us. "I know everyone here hates me for asking questions about Orly. But I need to know *why*. I mean, I showed up, and they put me in a room with him as though it was nothing. No one told me I was rooming with a boy. I don't know why no one understands that I can't feel comfortable with that. Didn't I have a right to be told? How am I supposed to feel safe if he pretends to be a girl but isn't?"

Of course, Soph responds to that. Her voice crackles with anger. "First of all, Orly is *not* a boy. You should stop saying that. Didn't you hear what she said downstairs?"

"Hey," I reach out, putting my hand on Soph's arm to calm her down. "We don't need to have a fight here." My hand misses Soph's arm and I feel what I think is her thigh. I pat it anyway. The Hennessy is definitely at work.

Soph turns her next question to Chris. Her breath brushes my face. "I wanna ask something. I wanna know if you asked your boyfriend why he broke up with you."

Chris's response is sharp. "No, I didn't. He hurt my feelings. It came out of the blue."

"Well, you can't 'vestigate someone unless you try talking to them. If you talked to Orly, you'd find out that she's totally nice." Soph has a point.

Chris isn't buying it, though. "I shouldn't have to ask about something like that. They should have told me. Same with Miguel. He shouldn't have just sent a five-word text. I blocked him after that."

"You rushed to judgment," Soph says. "Both times. Journalists are supposed to present both sides even if they think one is bullshit." Chris doesn't respond. I try a different approach.

"Chris, I get why you might have been—hey, you have to keep passing the bottle—thass—*that's* a rule." I reach over, and she lets me take it from her. I take another small sip and pass it back to Soph.

I try again. "Chris, you have to—I mean, I get you were surprised." My voice is sloppy. That sounds like "sprized" even to me. I take a breath and speak very slowly. "And maybe you're right, maybe Orly or the organizers should have asked you before they put you in a room with her, but what you did wasn't anything that made you safer from Orly, whazzit?"

I take the bottle from Soph and pass it back to Chris without drinking.

"What do you mean?" she asks sullenly.

"I mean, if you were worried about her doing something, you could have gone to Professor Forsythe or asked to switch rooms. Or you could have asked her why she didn't tell you. Maybe she was just as scared of you as you were of her." Chris starts to interrupt, but I keep talking. "Instead, you talked about her behind her back and decided to make her a news story. Then you refused to work with us on the group project so you could spy on her and write about it. How did that make you safer?"

Chris is silent. Soph reaches across me and takes the bottle from Chris. For some reason, her arm brushing up against my front makes me think I need to make the bottle passing rule clearer. But my stomach quakes, and I say, "You know you actually made both Orly and yourself less safe."

"How so?" Chris asks. I think she might be listening to me. I'm dizzy and I don't feel so good, but getting her to listen might be a really good idea.

"You made Orly less safe because you've been treating her like an outsider and encurrenced, I mean, *en-cour-aged* other people to. And you wouldn't even talk to her about it."

What I say next seems like a good idea until the words come out of my mouth. "And you made yourself less safe 'cause no one had your number tonight. You were missing and you could have been hurt. You were hiding in your room in a stupid ice storm, and no one had your number to text you because you don't have any friends here."

After I say that, I realize I'm about to throw up *right now*. I push the blankets off and try to get to the bathroom.

Chris is still silent, but I can hear Soph behind me say, softly, "Damn, Tess."

✳   ✳   ✳

From Soph Alcazar's Writing Journal,
February 14, 2018

A powerless night with three turns messy.
I'm surprised what comes out with Hennessy.

Chapter Eighteen

From the Fan Fiction Unbound Archive,
posted by conTessaofthecastle:

Daphne moved steadily through the forest, not letting herself think about anything but getting closer to the Portal of Arden. She wouldn't think about what had happened to Astoria. She wouldn't think about Lord Quintana, his dark eyes furious as he forbade Astoria from ever attempting the shape-shifting spell again. She wouldn't think of the coachman and his passenger, Lord Quintana's sister, frozen on the trail where she had bound them with the strongest spell she knew. She had used the unpredictable restraining spell her mother had warned her against. Even now she wasn't sure it would hold. She needed to hurry.

Soph.

TESS WAKES ME UP THE next morning, telling me, "Soph, we have to make breakfast."

It takes me a minute to figure out where I am. The room is still dark, and my head hurts. I remember last night and realize the power must still be out. My mouth is fuzzy, and I taste Hennessy, which makes me want to gag. "What time is it? God, how did you wake up?"

"Six-thirty. No one sleeps late on a dairy farm, Soph."

"It's freezing in here. Where's Chris?"

"I'm here," Chris groans from the floor, where she'd wrapped herself in our extra blankets and used Tess's pillow. She sits up groggily and asks, "What are we supposed to do now?"

"You can stay here, Chris, but Soph and I are supposed to go down and start breakfast for everyone."

"I'm taking a hot shower," Chris declares, and I hear Tess snort.

"Chris—no electricity, no pump, no water. Stay under your blanket."

Chris groans again and lies back down on the floor. I sit up and reach for a sweatshirt. Tess and I walk out into the dark hallway. "How are we supposed to make breakfast, then?"

"I don't know. It depends on what's in the kitchen. The stoves are gas, so they might work, but not the ovens." How can Tess be so awake?

"Let me put on something warm." My head is killing me.

Daylight is starting to creep through the window. Tess and I make our way downstairs to the kitchen. By now we can see what we're doing.

Tess's face is pale, and she's a little unsteady on her feet. She winces and groans as she pulls open the heavy door to the giant refrigerator.

"Are you okay?" I put out my hand to steady her. She looks down at my hand, and I take it back.

She looks at me and shrugs. "Headache."

"Do you want to go back to bed?" I ask. Screw breakfast. She looks as awful as I feel.

"Nope." She sticks her head in the dark refrigerator, and says, "I don't see anything in here except cold cuts and eggs."

"Those are from lunch yesterday. You said the roads would be bad. Do you think they couldn't make deliveries?"

"Probably. The fridge is still cold, so I guess the food's safe to eat. We could put out ham and cheese. There's eggs. Maybe we'll get lucky and the cooktop's gas."

I search the pantry and call out, "There are leftover hard rolls."

Tess comes over. "What's a hard roll?" I notice her accent when she says "hard." It's softer than what you hear on TV.

"You know, a hard roll." I hold the bag up for her to see.

Tess laughs and says, "Oh, you mean a bulkie."

"A what?"

"A bulkie roll. It's not hard."

I laugh. "We call it a hard roll, even though it's not hard. It's not as soft as a hamburger bun."

Tess smiles. "Who would want to eat bread called 'hard'? It sounds stale."

"No, it's good. We have them all the time in the morning. Hey! That's what we should do."

"What? Eat hard rolls?"

"No, make breakfast sandwiches."

"You mean like an Egg McMuffin?"

"No. Well, I guess. In the City, we buy them off food carts on the sidewalk. Hard rolls with eggs, cheese, ham, sausage, or bacon. They're all warm and melty. Everyone loves them! On the street, they come in aluminum foil."

"How are the eggs cooked?"

"I don't know. Scrambled I guess, or fried. You're the cook. We need to be able to pile the eggs onto the hard rolls with cheese and that leftover ham."

I can see that she's thinking. "I think I know how. Let's get everything going." She closes her eyes and takes a breath. I'm about to ask her if she's okay again, when she opens her eyes slowly and moves toward the drawers next to the ovens. "I'll find matches."

We hear people moving around outside the kitchen. Yin pokes her head in from the swinging door to the dining room. She's wrapped a blanket around her body. "What happened to you guys last night?" She yawns. "We didn't see you after you went on your rescue mission."

"Let me put it this way—my head is killing me, and I'm not sure I remember everything."

Yin laughs. "It sounds like more fun than the poetry slam! What are you doing with that bag of wecks?"

Tess looks up from the drawer and asks, "What's a weck?"

"You know, those things." Yin points at the bags of hard rolls. "Beef-on-weck is the official sandwich of Buffalo. It's delicious. Weck is short for *kimmelweck*."

I tell her, "Well, it's going to be breakfast-on-weck if we can figure out how." Yin smiles and withdraws to the dining room.

I follow Tess to the walk-in refrigerator. We take out the eggs, cheese, and all the leftover ham. Tess tells me to break three dozen eggs into a large mixing bowl. I start, but stop when I hear her let out a little shriek.

"Soph, you don't smash the eggs in the bowl. You'll drop shells in them." She laughs.

Sure enough, there are little bits of shell in the two eggs I broke into the bowl. I dump them down the drain and turn back to her. "You do it, then!" I snap. I'm cold, my head hurts, I can still taste Hennessy in the back of my mouth, and she should be able to tell I don't know how to cook.

"Let me show you how." Tess doesn't notice that I just lost my temper with her. And then she surprises me. She takes another egg and hands it to me, puts both of her hands over mine, and guides them over the bowl. She shows me how to crack the egg sharply on the side, and then uses her hands to help my hands pull the egg apart gently. Her hands are cold. "Tap, hold, and pull," she explains, and we do another one that way. Her hands warm as they cocoon mine. "Now you try." She steps back, and I almost protest, but I pick up a third egg and show her I can do it.

It takes a couple of tries, but I figure it out. By the time I'm through with three dozen eggs, I can do it without getting sticky. Between my headache and my earlier ineptitude, I don't want to give Tess any satisfaction, but I can't help being proud of myself. "Look—no shells." She grins at me.

While I've been cracking eggs, Tess has been cutting open hard rolls. Bulkie rolls. Whatever.

Janaye walks in, with a blanket still around her. "What's up with the Kaiser rolls, you guys? Are we ordering off the street cart this morning?"

"We're calling it a Power Outage Breakfast, Janaye," I say. "I'm cracking eggs like there's a big crowd coming to the diner!"

Tess comes over holding a large wiry thing with a handle. "Wait a minute," she says to Janaye. "I thought these were called hard rolls in New York. What's a Kaiser?"

Janaye and I grin at each other and shrug, and we both say "Brooklyn," at the same time.

Tess shakes her head when we start laughing. She hands the kitchen tool to me.

"Use this whisk to beat the eggs."

Janaye goes into the dining room to find Clover. Mixing the eggs is harder than it looks. The mixing tool is awkward and the eggs want to slip out of the bowl. But I finish and turn back to her. "Now what?"

She shows me a giant frying pan that is all shiny inside. "I greased this. We're going to pour the eggs in and scramble them. I got the pilot light on the stove top lit." She sees me staring. "Girl Scout. Gold Award. Remember?" She rolls her eyes at me, but smiles. "Go on, Soph. Pour the eggs in." After I do so, she puts the pan on the stove and asks me to find her a spatula. Once she's cooked the eggs, we assemble the sandwiches, with egg, ham, and cheese in each hard roll.

"Bulkie," she says stubbornly, but I see her grinning and can't help smiling back.

"Fine, you can say 'bulkie.' Unless you're going 'weck' or 'Kaiser.'" We both laugh. It's fun working together. Once we have three long rows of sandwiches, I ask, "Now what?"

"Are they done? Do they look right?"

She's asking me? I think for a minute. "I don't know. Let's try one."

I pick one up and take a bite. The bread is a little hard, almost stale. The cheese and ham are cold. "Something's not right. It's supposed to be soft and warm."

"What do you think is missing?"

Again, she's asking me? I try to picture the perfect breakfast sandwich, the one from the corner of Third Avenue and East 88th Street. I should be able to do this. I'm a poet! "Let me see. When we buy them, they do it all quickly, in this little metal cart and then when we unwrap them—oh, of course, we need to wrap them in foil and warm them up!"

"Great idea, Soph!" At first I think she's being sarcastic, but she means it. Maybe I *can* cook something after all.

The oven is dead, so we wrap all the sandwiches in foil and pile them into a huge soup pot. Tess puts them on the stove top, and fifteen minutes later we pile hot sandwiches on a tray. We can hear the other girls talking in the dining room.

Tess says, "Time to serve your breakfast bulkies, Soph." She's kidding, but I don't mind. "You take them in; I'll find paper plates."

I pick up the tray and as I open the door to the dining room, I hear a click and see the room grow bright. The power's back! I laugh at the timing. Most of the girls are standing around in the dining room, and someone claps.

Gabriela asks brightly, "What's for breakfast?"

I hear Tess behind me say, "Straight from the streets of New York City, egg sandwiches on hard rolls."

"What's a hard roll?" someone asks.

"Same thing as breakfast-on-weck. Tess, you tell them!" I say happily. I grab one and go upstairs to shower.

I'm on the way from our room to the shower when I see Grace in the hallway.

"Have you seen Chris?"

"No. She spent the night in our room, but she's not there now." I wonder what that's about.

Tess.

GRACE IS THE ONLY INSTRUCTOR at breakfast. She tells us to relax for a couple of hours and come back to the lounge at ten-thirty. Everyone goes back to their rooms to take long, hot showers. Soph finds ibuprofen in her bag and offers it for my headache. I take it with the glass of water she brings me and think about how much better we worked this morning than when we made that first meal. It was fun watching her figure out how to make the breakfast sandwiches taste the way they do in New York City, which she calls "the City," like it's the only one. Soph may be very different from me, but she is honestly excited about all kinds of things and she isn't afraid to show it. She's always willing to pitch in, even when she doesn't know how.

In the lounge, Grace tells us that Professor Forsythe and the others couldn't make it back last night because of the ice storm. Joan and Celestine were supposed to give a seminar, but, since they aren't around, we should work on our individual writing projects or with our groups. Soph is clearly disappointed. She was supposed to meet with Professor Forsythe alone this morning to go over her poems.

I'm thinking I'll work on my fan fic in our room, when I hear Soph's voice behind me on the stairs. "Tess, we're going stir crazy!"

She's with Janaye. They're both smiling. Janaye asks, "Since you're from around here. I thought you'd know something fun to do. I'm so sick of writing!"

I know what they mean. We've been working all week. "Is Grace still in the lounge?"

I go back down the stairs and look out the big window at the hill behind the lodge. It's still cold, which means the ice hasn't melted. It may be slippery outside, but that will actually help. I turn back to Soph and Janaye.

"Want to test your new boots and go sledding?"

Soph and Janaye both nod. I haven't seen any sleds here, but Janaye comes up with another idea.

"We used to take the trays from the school cafeteria over to the Park and use them. The school hated it because they lost them, but it was fun. There're plenty of trays here."

Soph is perplexed. "You guys took trains all the way from Brooklyn to Central Park with cafeteria trays?"

Janaye rolls her eyes. "No, *princesa*, Prospect Park has skating *and* sledding!"

Of course, I couldn't tell you where either park is, but the idea of taking sleds of any sort on a subway makes me laugh. Soph laughs too. Janaye goes to the kitchen to scout trays. I go upstairs to tell the other girls.

Soph follows close behind and asks, "Are you going to invite…" I wince. Even though I had too much to drink last night, I remember what I said to Chris. She never came down to breakfast this morning. That's on me.

I cut Soph off before she mentions Chris's name. "We're not excluding anyone. I'll go let them know." And so I go tell everyone on our floor, and then I climb up to the third floor where Chris has found another room. But she isn't there when I stick my head in. On the way back down the stairs, I see her talking with Grace in one of the little rooms off the lounge. Before Grace closes the door, I get a glimpse of Chris. I think she's crying.

❋   ❋   ❋

From Soph Alcazar's Writing Journal,
February 15, 2018

Our breakfast challenge, "great idea," she says.
We laugh at hard rolls, bulkies, Kaisers, wecks.
Janaye then teaches us to sled using trays.
I notice Chris, she won't let us forget.

Chapter Nineteen

From the Fan Fiction Unbound Archive,
posted by con Tessaofthecastle:

The sunset that night burned brightly in every color. Daphne reached a clearing on a rocky hill. She didn't even notice the sky stretched in front of her, deepening into vibrant shades of orange, purple, and blue. The Portal of Arden lay below. She didn't take her eyes off it as she walked. She was so exhausted she wasn't even sure what she was walking toward anymore, the Portal, Astoria, the spell-caster. They all blended in her mind and she knew only that she couldn't stay where she was. There was a small house halfway down the hill. Stumbling wearily, she looked to see if there was a haystack or a barn she could hide in for the night.

Soph.

TESS REMINDS ME OF SOMETHING Gordon once said about Lally. "She doesn't have a mean bone in her." I think she knew I was going to say not to ask Chris. After last night, who needs the tension? But she's right. Janaye was right, too, that Tess would know something to do. It was fun making dinner with her the other night, and she was a decent drinking buddy last night. Maybe she isn't all that serious.

Orly is in the lounge, and I poke my head in to ask if she wants to go with us. She smiles and shakes her head. "The teachers found out about Chris and her carrot. I understand that Grace is about to make Chris apologize to me. I reckon I should stick around and see how that goes."

By the time we make it to the kitchen there are eight of us, including Yin, Gabriela, and Peggy. Tess puts her finger to her mouth to tell us to keep quiet as we sneak into the kitchen to take the trays from the dishwashing rack. Then we edge along the far wall of the dining room so that Grace won't see us.

The sun is finally out. Ice coats the snow, and we make crunching sounds stepping through it as we tramp behind the lodge to a hill. At the top, Janaye yells, "Like this." She takes a running start holding the tray in front of her, drops it, jumps on it, and rides it down the slope on her knees.

Everyone else goes ahead, until I'm alone at the top. Tess is at the bottom of the hill; her pink jacket sets her apart from the other girls. I pause, watching her. Then I remember Joey and I jump on the tray I'm holding and slide down the slope.

When we sneak back into the lodge later in the afternoon, we find Professor Forsythe, Joan, and Celestine sitting in the lounge with Grace.

Celestine says, "Make sure all those trays find their way back to the racks, please." Before I can apologize, I see Celestine smile and wink broadly to show they aren't mad.

I stop to ask Orly how the apology went. She rolls her eyes and says she doesn't want to talk about it.

Tess.

AFTER DINNER TONIGHT, THEY SHOW a bunch of TED talks by women authors. I'm bored until Soph leans over and whispers in my ear, "Let's go outside." She and Orly tiptoe out. I take a look around, but no one is paying attention. Clover and Janaye are in the lounge having a debate about whether graphic novels count as real literature, so the three of us run up the stairs, grab our coats and snow boots, and run back outside.

It's dark and the stars seem fluid, there are so many. "Are we going to make snow angels?"

Orly asks what they are.

"We'll show you," Soph assures her. "We stand together, lie on our backs in the snow, and wave our arms so the impressions in the snow make angels' wings."

We find a clear patch of snow and lie down on our backs. Orly gasps when she feels the cold through her clothing. Then we jump back up, and when she sees the three identical angels side by side under the moonlight, Orly smiles. Soph and I stand on either side of her and we each touch one of her arms.

"You can't tell who's who," says Orly. It's clear she likes that.

"No," I say, "and snow angels always wear robes, so when I was little I thought they were all girls, even when boys were making them. They're another kind of snowsister, I guess."

"How long will they last?" Orly asks.

"Oh, they'll—we'll—probably be filled in with fresh snow before the weekend."

"But we'll still be there together, under the snow, even if no one can see us?"

"At least until there's a thaw," I tell her. I misunderstand what she means.

But Soph gets it. "Even when no one can see us," she says. "Even when we've gone home and we're far away from each other."

We're quiet. Faint noises come from the lodge behind us, and people move in the lighted rooms. The sky is close and cold.

Finally, Orly announces, "Okay, girls, the weather's too much for this Georgia pecan," and goes back inside.

Soph wants to stay, and I do too, with her, the girl from another world. We decide to walk around to the back of the lodge and visit the original snowsisters.

It's the kind of cold that makes your feet squeak when you walk, and we can see our breath as we go. My fingers stiffen inside my fleece gloves. I shove them in my pockets to warm them up. I can feel the cold all down my legs where my jeans got wet from lying down.

"New Hampshire is really beautiful," Soph says, stopping on the shoveled path and looking up. "You never see this many stars in the City. Too bad I'll never get into Minerva now."

I look up, too. It's nice, being out here, just the two of us. I decide to ask her something, since we're alone.

"Soph, what you said earlier this week about playing follow-the-leader." Her breath comes out in clouds. "Did you mean it about me being a leader?"

"Totally." She shrugs. "Why would I say it if I didn't mean it? Do you think I'm some kind of phony?" She sounds more surprised than mad.

"I don't know. No." I'm going out on a limb. At least no one else is outside. My heart thumps, although that could be from the cold. "People say a lot of things they don't mean."

She's genuinely curious now and asks, "What do *you* mean?"

I focus on my boots in the snow. *I can't do this. I want to do this. I can't do this. Joey, can I do this?*

Apparently, Soph realizes I'm trying to figure something out, because she asks me her own question without waiting for me to answer. "You stuck up for Orly. You even stuck up for Chris. Did you mean *that?*"

"Of course I did," I say, indignant that she would question that.

"Well," she draws out the word, and pushes her wool beanie back from her forehead, "I mean, you're a pretty conservative girl."

She must see my confused expression, because she keeps talking quickly.

"I don't mean that in a bad way, Tess. Really. You know, you wear all these pink feminine clothes and you go to church. You're going into the military. You get your boyfriend's approval for most of what you do. You talk to him every day, as if you have to check in with him, and so I wonder—"

I interrupt her.

"I don't have a boyfriend."

"But—" She's confused. "But you told me about him. And you text him all the time. Today, you texted him again, this morning. You said—"

"He's not my boyfriend, Soph."

"But you said—" She's genuinely confused now. *I can do this. I want to do this.*

I cut her off. "It's a long story. He needs a girlfriend. We're friends. I need to do this for him."

She shakes her head and walks ahead of me. I struggle to catch up with her on the narrow path. She turns and we face each other.

"I'm lost. How come he gets a girlfriend but you don't get a boyfriend?"

"No, Soph… I'm not his girlfriend. And I don't want a boyfriend."

"Then *you* didn't mean what *you* said, but you're saying you didn't believe me? Tess, I'm still lost. And I'm back to wondering about you defending Orly and Chris."

Soph's face is flushed, and she stares at me. She's mad now. Her mouth is slightly open. Her lips look wet. I think to myself, *I can't do this.*

"Tess, can you explain, please?"

I reach for her arm and pull her to me. She stumbles forward stiffly, and I kiss her, faster than I expected to, but slower than I imagined it would be. I feel her lips tighten at first and then relax. The next thing you know she is kissing me back; her mouth is warm and soft on mine. The nighttime air is cold around us, but I can feel the heat radiating from her.

Then she pulls away from me, turns quickly, and walks back to the lodge without saying a word.

⁂ ⁂ ⁂

From Soph Alcazar's Writing Journal,
February 15, 2018

We three step out, make angels in the snow.
She kissed me! What the devil do I know?

Chapter Twenty

From the Fan Fiction Unbound Archive,
posted by con Tessaofthecastle:

Market Day in Arden was crowded. The shouts of the vendors blended with shoppers as Daphne made her way to the central square. Suddenly she felt a hand on her arm. Struggling to release herself and jostled by the crowd, Daphne found herself momentarily unable to breathe. She had come this far. If she was forced to return to the Coven now, before she had mastered the space-shifting spell, before she found Astoria, both of them would be lost forever.

Soph.

SO THAT WAS UNEXPECTED. SHOCKING, in fact. Without thinking, I walk back to the lodge. I make it to the room—our room— without having to talk to anyone except Janaye, who sees me in the hallway and wants to chat. I wave her off. I am overheated after the cold outside, and the layers on me feel heavy and constricting.

I pull clothing off, my hat and gloves, then my jacket and the scarf I have wrapped around my neck. I sit on the bed and fumble with my shoelaces. God, these boots are so clumsy and heavy. I'm breathing heavily. My fingers are stiff and useless, and I realize my eyes are filling with tears.

Tess opens the door. I keep my head down, but I can see her boots out of the corner of my eye. I have the ridiculous thought that her boots are knock-offs, not "the Original L.L.Bean Maine Hunting Shoes." This is stupid. I abandon my laces and stand.

"Why did you do that?" My voice sounds thin and shaky. *Goddamnit.* She stands in the doorway like some perfect china doll with her long hair flowing out of that little pink hat, cheeks pink from the cold, mouth open a little. Her face is serious, and I realize that she has tears in her eyes too.

None of this makes any sense. I sit on the bed again, and stare back at her. Now I'm getting mad again.

"My first girl kiss, and you ruined it. I'm not a guinea pig for you to experiment on, you know. Why did you do that if you didn't mean it?"

She steps into the room, pulls the door closed, and locks it. Meeting my gaze, her voice barely above a whisper, she says, "I *did* mean it."

Now I am completely confused. The silence hangs in the air between us until I wipe my eyes, which are wet with the damn tears. I bend down to work on my laces again. I want nothing more than to get these boots off my feet.

She speaks again. "Can I tell you about Joey?"

I don't want to know why she is cheating on her boyfriend or her not-boyfriend. I shake my head and keep working on the laces on my left boot. The double knot is tight and my fingers aren't much warmer.

"He's not my boyfriend." Her voice is quiet, almost a whisper. She stammers, "He, he's gay."

I pause and then I turn back to that double knot, attacking it as if it is the SAT math section.

Tess speaks again, her voice still a whisper. "So am I."

I straighten and stare at her again, hard. She looks terrified, which I don't understand. That infuriates me.

I stand again, still in the damn boots, and glare at her. "What, you hate yourself for being gay? You pretend to be straight to convince yourself and everyone else in your redneck town that you're something you aren't? Does that make you feel good? Or normal?" Time for a new roommate. I can go bunk with Orly.

I grab my room key from the nightstand and head straight toward Tess, expecting her to move out of the way and let me through the door. She doesn't move. I am inches from her, about to push her out of the way, when she says, "Joey. When he tried to come out, he got his jaw broken."

I am so close to her I can hear her breathing. She is really crying now and puts her face in her hands. My stomach drops.

"Oh." Gently, stumbling in these stupid boots, I guide her over to her bed and sit us both down. She stares at the floor. I rub my hands together, unsure what to do.

"Didn't he tell someone?" I ask after a pause. "Get the police involved? Sue? I mean, even in New Hampshire you can't break someone's jaw for being gay. It must be a hate crime."

"He couldn't tell anyone." Her voice is tiny now, and I can see tears coursing silently down her cheeks. I reach out to wipe them off with my thumb. The gesture startles her, and she flinches. I withdraw my hand.

When I speak again, I try to keep my voice level, even though I want to shake her.

"Tess, he needs to tell someone. It's against the law to hit someone. And to hurt someone for being gay. His parents can—"

She grabs the hand I used to wipe her tears and squeezes it hard.

"It was his father who broke his jaw, Soph."

Tess

LATER, WHEN I GO HOME and try to remember what happened after I said that, I will have a hard time with the details and I'll finally give up trying to recall all of it. I won't remember the few words Soph says, or her face when she gathers me into her arms and holds us together for long moments. I smell her citrusy soap and feel her hair, vaguely ticklish against my face. She gets up and double-checks the lock on the door. I've never seen her go this long without talking. And I can't focus on watching her because of the tears in my eyes, but after she checks the lock she moves one of the nightstands in front of the door, and then turns off the overhead light and comes back to me in the dark.

The window lets in moonlight until she lowers the blind, still not speaking. Then she unzips my jacket, like I'm a small child. She bends down to undo her boots first, then mine, peeling layers of cold, wet clothing off of me while I sit there, almost motionless.

I find my voice before she finds hers, as she is pulling the socks off my feet. She's already got me out of my jeans, somehow, and I'm in my sweater and underwear shivering. "I'm sorry," I say so softly that even I can barely hear it. "I just really wanted to kiss you." I can feel a fresh wave of tears about to start, when she looks up from the floor at me.

She starts to smile, but then catches herself, and asks, "Just because I'm a girl?"

"No," I tell her, "not just because you're a girl. Because you're amazing. But I didn't mean to ruin your first kiss."

She doesn't say anything, just turns back to my socks. But then she says the last thing I expect her to. "You didn't ruin it, Tess. I mean, it's not ruined anymore." After that, she tips her head up and kisses me. I *will* remember that.

We end up under the covers in her bed, pressed together with the cold seeping from our limbs. I try to tell her I'm not confused about liking girls and I'm definitely not confused about liking *her*, but I need to keep it to myself for now. I end up saying something jumbled and confused. Apparently, it's okay, because she kisses me again. She says something, but it isn't clear and it doesn't matter.

The details are fuzzy, but I will never forget how, close to Soph that night, finally warm, entangled with her under the heavy covers, my face pushed into the crook of her neck, I fall off to sleep, feeling something I would never in my whole life have expected to feel at that moment—completely and entirely safe.

✳ ✳ ✳

From Soph Alcazar's Writing Journal,
February 15, 2018

I thought that the closet was the worst crime.
But there's more to it, my very first time.

Chapter Twenty-One

From the Fan Fiction Unbound Archive,
posted by conTessaofthecastle:

As Daphne pulled more forcefully against the stranger gripping her arm, she caught a whiff of the scent that had been haunting her: roses and ash. Astoria was here, pulling at her arm. Before anyone could stop her, Daphne grabbed the hand and uttered the space-shifting incantation, "Actessar."
Everything went black.

Soph.

I'M THE FIRST TO WAKE up and I try not to wake Tess. I'm lying on my side nestled against her back; my arm is around her waist. I can hear her breathing, and her hair tickles my face. I feel a smile spread across my face, one of those big, dopey grins. Last night wasn't like I expected, but it was still great! I want to stay here for as long as possible. We are very far from anywhere familiar to me. Even though the room is cold outside the blankets, I feel warm and cozy, protective and loving. I never want it to end.

I run over what happened this week: Chris and fan fiction, skating with Orly, Tess with the carrot; making dinner and breakfast; drinking in the dark; Tess kissing me under a million stars. I feel bad that I made Tess cry. And I wonder about Joey.

How could his own father break his jaw? What does Tess's family think? Are they all barbarians up here? Freddy's got nothing to worry about compared to Joey.

Tess stirs, and I feel her stiffen next to me. She straightens, and I am cold where our bodies were touching but now aren't. She turns onto her back; her eyes blink open, still heavy with sleep, the green flecks in them almost catlike. She smiles tentatively. I smile back and put my arm across her stomach, thinking this means we're "side by each." We say the same thing at the same time. "I've never…"

"I didn't think you were… But you are. I'm glad."

"I'm glad *you* are."

I roll forward, so that my shoulder is over hers but I'm not on top of her. I turn my head so that my chin touches her neck and my nose is in her hair.

Tess speaks first. "So, I guess you came out to everyone in New York?"

"Yes. Of course." Then I realize I shouldn't presume anything. "Well, not everyone. I didn't take out an ad in the *Times* or anything. I mean, me being gay isn't a big deal for my family and school. October 11 is National Coming Out Day. I already told my friends, Gordon and Lally and Mibs. Two years ago, Gordon and I both came out at school that day and then went home and told our parents. Lally came out this year. She's ace." I'm nervous that I will say the wrong thing. "Doesn't anyone else know about you, Tess? I mean, besides Joey?"

Tess shifts. "Just Joey." She pauses. "You think that's bad. I know." She sighs. I slide my hand from her stomach to her hip and pull her toward me.

"No, I… Well… You know, it's better to come out, Tess. Everyone is safer if we all come out and find each other. Don't you want to live without having to keep that secret?"

She sits erect, sliding herself up against the headboard, forcing my hand away from her waist. She rubs her face with her hands, and then, without looking at me, she says in a low voice, "Soph, it's not safe for *me*. My town is not safe. I told you, Joey, his father…" Her voice trails off.

"What happened, Tess?" I'm still lying on the pillow. I'm not sure what to do with my hands, so I pull them back and tuck them under my arms. Her hair is mussed, and all I want to do is run my fingers through it and kiss her again. But I don't.

"If I tell you, Soph, it has to stay between us. Tomorrow you're going back to New York and I'm going back to the farm, but you can't tell *anyone*. I shouldn't be telling *you*, even."

"I understand. I'll keep it to myself." I had forgotten we're leaving tomorrow. Her saying that pushes all the air out of my lungs.

"Joey and I have always been friends. We went to preschool together. He told me he thought he was gay in ninth grade. And I told him… well, I was figuring stuff out myself. We pretty much knew we couldn't tell anyone." She stares at the ceiling while she says this, but she knows I'm looking at her.

"Joey's father drinks and he has a bad temper. Joey tries to stay out of his way as much as he can. He always has. But last year, his dad caught Joey on the computer. I don't know what Joey had on it. He wouldn't tell me. But his father caught him and accused him of being gay. Joey denied it at first, but his father told him to be a man whatever he was and then asked him if he was gay. Joey didn't answer, but then finally he said he thought he was. His father took a swing at him and said he wouldn't have any," Tess's voice catches, "f-fags in his house." Her chin quivers, as if she's going to start crying again.

I reach for her hand, squeezing it tightly in her lap. "Oh, Tess."

"Joey didn't want to do anything about it, but he couldn't move his jaw. He texted me from the emergency room. His dad drove him to the hospital and left him there. I could barely understand what happened when he tried to explain it. He told them in the emergency room that he fell down the stairs at my house. If he didn't, Soph, the police would have gotten involved, and I can only guess what Joey's father would have done. They had to wire his mouth shut. He had to wear one of those collars, too, because his father sprained Joey's neck with that punch.

"I was afraid for Joey to go back to his home, but his mom came to pick him up and take him. They wouldn't let him leave without a parent. His mom didn't say anything to the people in the emergency room. Joey's father acted as if nothing had happened. He was sixteen, Soph. He had no place to go. He still doesn't. He doesn't have any money or any other family he can live with. So, we figured out that we could be boyfriend and girlfriend for now. If we acted that way, his dad would leave him alone, and Joey would be safe until he left home."

I squeeze her hand and start to speak, but she interrupts me.

"You don't understand it, Soph. I know." She says it matter-of-factly, not as if she's mad. "Joey and I don't have anyone else to talk to. We researched it on the Internet. I know there are schools with openly gay students, even public schools. Gay characters are on TV now and not just as a joke or mentally ill. But Joey and I also looked up what gay teens should do. We need to keep ourselves safe, and that means not coming out until we are in a safe place. Joey's home," she pauses, "maybe my home, too, they are not safe. Our town is not safe." She takes a ragged breath and is quiet. Then she adds, "We don't have gay clubs at school or youth groups or LGBTQ community centers in Castleton. We don't talk about this kind of thing. My family isn't going to be happy if they find out. My MeMe…" her voice trails off.

"Isn't there *some* place that you could go?" I ask. It makes no sense to me that in this day and age they have to fake a relationship.

"No, Soph, there isn't." Her voice is flat with resignation. "I know New York is different. But not everyone gets to be from a big city where no one cares about this kind of thing. And even in big cities bad things happen, like that shooting in Florida. Don't you know that people like us…?" She pauses as if she doesn't want to say the words. "Kids often end up homeless because they have to escape their families? They run away because home isn't safe. Some of them kill themselves, Soph." Her voice is soft.

Hearing this, I realize that I haven't spent much time thinking about it before now. "Tess, I'm sorry. I *did* know that. I've read it too. I didn't think… Well, it doesn't seem real to me. I guess, I mean it *didn't* seem real. I've never known anyone in that kind of danger." Without meaning to, I begin to cry. "I'm so, so sorry, Tess."

She continues, in her quiet, calm voice, and I feel her begin to rub my back gently, in small, even strokes.

"Next year I'll either be in West Point, if I can make it in, or I'll have enlisted. I can come out there. And maybe my family will be okay with that. I don't really know." She stops talking.

"Are you sure, Tess? I looked up stuff about women in the military and then gays, and it looked scary to me."

"I know the military has problems," Tess says in that calm voice, "but it's the best option for me. I know it isn't always going to be easy. But, Soph, it's a free education. And then a job. It's my only chance to go somewhere other than the farm—to see different places, try to do things differently than they do at home. Maybe if my family sees me trying to do my best—" She catches herself, then starts again. "My dad says, 'if you work hard, the army will reward you.' I know I can work hard. I just need a chance to prove myself." She shrugs. "Maybe I can change some people's opinions. Maybe if I do a good job, I can even win a few fans." I smile at her joke.

Tess is serious and thoughtful, unlike most girls our age. At first, I thought that she was old-fashioned. Then I started to think she was just conservative. Then I was just shocked that she's gay and disappointed that she's in the closet. But now I understand. She isn't in denial. She has a plan. She's strategic.

She'll keep quiet now and she and Joey will be safe. I think she must be using her fan fiction writing to organize her feelings without having to tell anyone she's writing it. It's a lot to consider, and I don't much want to think about any of it. The feel of her hand on my back makes me want to go back under the covers with her and block out the world.

Tess withdraws her hand and turns on her side. I turn on my side, too, so that we're facing each other. She reaches her arm out to me. I pull the covers back up over us, close my eyes, and lean into her. She feels soft and warm. She also feels fragile, like that expensive Danish china my mother's always telling me not to use; but I know now that underneath, Tess isn't all that fragile. She pushes her forehead close to mine.

"It's—it's a hard world, Soph. It's hard for everyone in different ways." She kisses me again.

Tess.

I AM SURE I FIGURE out before Soph does how little time we have left. Soph is so optimistic, it wouldn't occur to her that we might be on borrowed time. This morning we're going to review our group projects with the faculty and then, after lunch, there's a peer review of our individual writing. Tonight is the final banquet, and tomorrow we go on a tour of Minerva College in the morning, everyone does a final reading of their individual work after lunch, and then we leave.

I don't say anything, even though I find it really hard to climb out of that bed, put on clothes, and leave the privacy of our room. As we're getting dressed, my cheeks heat up, knowing Soph's watching me. I put on my fleece pullover, then look down at it. Pink, like most of my clothes. I pull it off again and throw it on the bed, then draw in a deep breath for courage and ask Soph, "Can I borrow your sweater? The black one you wore the first night?" Soph is confused at first, then smiles. No, she grins broadly, like a kid at Christmas. She rummages through her bag. When she finds the sweater at the bottom, she throws it to me.

"Why black today, Tess?"

I shrug as I pull it over my head. It smells like a mixture of her citrusy soap and her, "I don't like pink that much," I say, and that startles her.

"Tess, your whole wardrobe is pink. Why do you wear it if you don't like it?" Her hands are frozen on the button of her jeans, and she's clearly perplexed. Yeah, I imagine Miss "Have my new boots overnight-shipped from L.L.Bean" wouldn't understand. Funny, today I find that endearing, whereas last night it was irritating.

"Because Mom buys my clothes and her choices are either Walmart or JC Penney. I don't care and, even if I did, no one would listen to me. This is what we wear in Castleton." That's something I never would have said to Soph when we first met.

"But…" She's still confused about something, I can tell. She's obviously trying not to make assumptions, which I think is harder for her than she realizes. Finally, she spits it out. "But what about the pink nail polish?"

I inspect my fingers; the shell pink Molly painted on them the day I left is starting to chip. I shrug and say, "My little sister likes to paint my nails."

She laughs and comes over to fiddle with the sweater, though really, it's to kiss me again. She says the sweater looks good on me, and then we turn to go down to breakfast. And it gets awkward once more.

Soph grabs my hand and starts out the door, and I have to pull my hand out of hers and shake my head at her. "Soph, please? I can't tell anyone."

She freezes instantly. She starts to try to convince me, but stops herself, puts her hand in her pocket, and walks out the door in front of me. She's silent until we sit down in the breakfast room and she says good morning to Orly. I feel mean and small and guilty, but I turn to Keisha and smile at her when she asks me if I slept all right. Soph and I don't say another word to each other for the entire meal.

✳   ✳   ✳

From Soph Alcazar's Writing Journal,
February 16, 2018

A father who could break his own son's jaw.
I've only read about the bad things they saw.

Chapter Twenty-Two

From the Fan Fiction Unbound Archive,
posted by con Tessaofthecastle:

*Daphne opened her eyes cautiously. The noise and the
pulsating wind gusts from the space-shifting spell died away
as she looked around. She was in the little house on the hillside
outside the Portal of Arden, where she had stopped the night
before.*

Soph.

I DON'T GET IT. TESS and I, we should be able to hold hands here.
No one's going to tell her family. Joey's father will never know.
Last night, this morning, I thought she was perfect for me; now
I think we're too different and she'll never catch up. So we head
down to breakfast, and I sit somewhere else. I want to talk about
it with someone and I bet Orly would understand. But I can't
tell her, of course. I owe that to Tess.

I go over to Orly anyway, noticing that she's sitting between
Janaye and Gabriela. I sit next to Gabriela and listen to them
talk. I'm relieved to hear that they are talking about their writing.
Janaye's tone is warm and interested.

I don't see Chris. But I don't want to think about Chris now.
I'm thinking about Tess, when she told me her home and her

town weren't safe. She was resigned, but I'm mad about it. I also remember Mom telling me to be safe before I left New York. I didn't agree with what she was trying to tell me. But now she's starting to make more sense.

I look across the table at Tess. She won't look at me. I wish she didn't look so good in my sweater.

Tess.

THAT MORNING IN THE FINAL group session, Keisha, Peggy, and I are all at a loss for words. We have a story about Maizy Donovan finding out her chief editor, George Golden, isn't paying her the same amount of money as the male reporters. Ultraman can't do anything to help her by using his superpowers, but only by standing up for her and telling the chief editor that her work is just as valuable as the men's. We have screenshots of the old comic strip to illustrate it and the whole thing is pretty good. Except it's not the assignment we were given. I emailed the whole thing to Chris last night, mostly because I thought I should. She never answered. Celestine finishes with another group and comes to sit down, and I figure this is when we're going to have to come clean. But just as Celestine is pulling out her chair, Chris comes across the room and drops down at the table.

"Hey," she says, "sorry to be late. I just finished up Maizy's undercover investigative piece and I emailed it to everyone."

Sure enough, Peggy pulls up our piece, to which Chris has added a whole section, complete with screenshots of the actual transcripts from a real court case about pay inequality from the 1970s.

I don't have any idea what to say. Neither does Peggy. Even Keisha is surprised. Celestine looks from one of us to the others. Then Chris starts talking as though she's been working with us all along.

"So, I wanted to use Tess's idea of having Maizy be involved in something that happened at the beginning of the comic strip, but I wanted to work on a real investigative news story. I did some online research and found out that in the early 1970s, a group of women reporters at *Newsweek* magazine discovered that they were being underpaid compared to the male reporters. They sued the magazine for an increase in their salaries. I did all the research on the case and wrote it up for Maizy to give to Mr. Golden. I think it ties in nicely with Keisha's explanation of the working environment for women at that time and with Peggy's descriptions. It let me go into the history of a real news story and do some solid background research. Did y'all know that *Newsweek* was owned by a woman and she ended up settling the case because she didn't want to come across as a hypocrite?"

Celestine asks a few questions, but she's excited about how the piece came out, and she tells us what a good job we did of meshing our different writing strengths.

"I wasn't sure you four would end up on the same page," she says, before she goes to meet with another group. "I'm pleased that you were able to put aside your differences and work together in the end."

After she leaves, no one knows what to say. Then I pull my phone out of my pocket. "Can I get your number?" I ask Chris.

Tom Wilinsky & Jen Sternick

✳   ✳   ✳

*From Soph Alcazar's Writing Journal,
February 16, 2018*

*Is nothing what I understand or think?
I'm wrong about so much, even the pink.*

Chapter Twenty-Three

From the Fan Fiction Unbound Archive,
posted by con Tessaofthecastle:

Astoria stood in front of Daphne. The hood of her heavy cape was flung back to show her golden hair, unmistakable anywhere. She held a mug of some steaming beverage in her hand. "You're home," Astoria said. She carefully set down the mug and came closer.

Soph.

I'm relieved to be with my group for the final session this morning. I like the way our piece came out. The ballad is a hodgepodge, with stanzas by each of us, in our respective styles. We adapted the story of Freya, who cried golden tears when her husband Od disappeared. In the real myth—duh, oxymoron— Freya put on her magical cloak and flew around the earth to find him. When she discovered that he'd been banished and turned into a sea monster, she stayed by him to console him. But he got killed, and Freya was so pissed off that she threatened to kill the other gods until they put her husband into Valhalla, their heaven for warriors. We made Freya marry both a husband and a wife. She meets Od early and he puts her amber necklace of love, the *Brísingamen*, on his own neck to make Freya fall in love and marry him. On her wedding night, she meets another goddess, Stola, and they instantly fall for each other without the Brísingamen. Od is inconsolable and runs away. Although the Brísingamen effect has worn off, Freya misses Od and uses her feather cloak to change into a bird and find him. She intends to use the Brísingamen to bind Stola to Od, but when she introduces Stola and Od, they find themselves attracted to each other without it and they throw a three-person wedding. Freya has children with Od and romantic love with Stola, the moral being that, in relationships, you offer different things and obtain different things from different people.

Gabriela, Yin, and Ellen each took the voice of a character, and I got the narration stanzas, because we agreed that my formal style worked better for me as a storyteller than as a participant.

When we show Grace the whole thing, she brings Professor Forsythe over.

I hope that Professor Forsythe likes it. I've almost given up on her, but Professor Forsythe is still my best hope for getting into Minerva College next year. The week is almost over, and still she hasn't seen anything I've written. I like the way she speaks to us as a group; she isn't casual, but she never lectures from a podium or with notes. She says smart things, from the heart and the mind combined. I've even forgiven her for forgetting everyone's names at first.

So, when Professor Forsythe puts on her rimless reading glasses and begins to read "Freya Reimagined," I'm on the edge of my seat with my legs jiggling. Yin nudges me as if to say, "What are you, five?" I put my hands in my lap and lean back, holding my legs still. I watch Professor Forsythe's face, her brow furrowing and relaxing, her mouth pursing, then smiling.

"Marvelous. Creative. Funny, but you have a real point here. I see Homer and Swift, but also some Steinem and, well, who's the comedian it recalls? Maybe Ellen DeGeneres. And from what we've seen and read from each of you, you've played to your strengths stylistically in your individual voices." I swear she looks at me for a split second. Then she continues. "I have to move on to the other groups now, but I recommend that you each think about why your own style works in each role and contrast it with each other's styles." She leans back and smiles. "I wonder if you'd like to read it aloud after dinner. It would be a nice way to cap our final night."

I'm so excited that I can barely wait for the break to text my friends.

[FROM SOPH TO GORDON, LALLY, AND MIBS] *Great news!!!*

This time, all three are around.

[FROM GORDON TO LALLY, MIBS, AND SOPH] *Wutz her name?*

[FROM SOPH TO GORDON, LALLY, AND MIBS] *Not that.*

[FROM GORDON TO LALLY, MIBS, AND SOPH] *Then wut?*

[FROM SOPH TO GORDON, LALLY, AND MIBS] *Group project so good we're reading it to everyone 2night.*

[FROM LALLY TO GORDON, MIBS, AND SOPH] *U Rock.*

Mibs sends a smiley face.

[FROM GORDON TO LALLY, MIBS, AND SOPH] *Wutz up with the other things?*

This brings me back to earth. I want to tell them about Tess. I could use the support. But I can't explain.

[FROM SOPH TO GORDON, LALLY, AND MIBS] *Nothing much.*

❋   ❋   ❋

AT LUNCH, TESS AND I steer clear of each other. Last night was so great. So was this morning before breakfast. I thought we connected in so many ways. Is Tess ashamed of me? Herself? Us? I want to say something, but I can't in the dining room or the lounge. I'll have to wait until tonight. We have a few minutes before the group session, so I take out my phone to text my friends, but none of them responds. I decide to try Freddy.

[FROM SOPH TO FREDDY] *Hey—you there? How was the bunny slope?*

Freddy responds right away.

[FROM FREDDY TO SOPH] *Awesome—did what you said. Instructor was *nice*.*

[FROM SOPH TO FREDDY] *Now what?*

[FROM FREDDY TO SOPH] *Wut?*

[FROM SOPH TO FREDDY] *What happens now?*

[FROM FREDDY TO SOPH] *Dunno. Best ski vacay ever. Even parents are happy.*

[FROM SOPH TO FREDDY] *Do they know?*

It takes Freddy a few minutes to respond.

[FROM FREDDY TO SOPH] *No. Not going there.*

How can Freddy stand this? Tess has a hostile home, and Joey's father, well he sounds creepy and scary. Freddy's parents should be able to handle it. They're in the City where anything goes. After the initial surprise, Mrs. Peckett would probably be thrilled that her son is gay.

[FROM SOPH TO FREDDY] *What do U need, F?*

[FROM FREDDY TO SOPH] *Not the third degree.*

Back at the table, Professor Forsythe talks about the peer review. "We'll take an hour and a half so that each person can read and think about the work they've received. If anyone wants to, they can discuss the work with the author quietly so as not to disturb the group. You should use this chance to inform your understanding of what the author is trying to say."

"Tomorrow, after we come back from touring Minerva, each of you will present to the group your final work and the person you've exchanged with today will comment on it. You should be prepared to describe it. Then your partner will explain what she thinks of it in a constructive manner."

✳ ✳ ✳

I LIKE GABRIELA, BUT HER poetry is very different from mine. She writes about loss with a stilted rhyme scheme and a fluid structure. I like the way she staggers lines of different lengths and she uses language that comes across as natural. Her poetry is about her father dying when she was young. She has a couple of lines about her mother which I don't understand. I tell her it should be clearer, and she ducks her head. We talk about it for a while.

I give Gabriela my Spenserian sonnet. It's the first time I've been able to mix up the lines like this and have them make sense together.

I could see the world as wide, bright and full,
Though without companionship, was alone.
With optimism, feeling, capable,

Love I'd find, corporeal, flesh and bone.

But first I learnt the limits of my zone
Of vision. I don't see all that is there.
My knowledge, my beliefs, what I have known,
I can expand if she will only share.

This world's not right, us, a clandestine pair,
Confined, contained, shut up in our small room.
If concealed even here, can anywhere
There be a place for us to finally bloom?

I don't know if the dark can be endured.
I wish I could see us both assured.

Gabriela reads it with her brow furrowed. "I don't think I understand, Soph. I see that it follows that pattern, but I'm not sure I understand it or agree with it. What are you saying?"

I'm disappointed. I was excited for her to read it. "I was trying to create a character who is optimistic, but finds someone who is too scared to be open about their relationship. It makes the protagonist doubt whether she can stay with them."

"Why?"

"Well, you know! If you keep something secret, that means you're ashamed." I'm surprised.

"Always?"

"Yes. Always."

"But can't there be good reasons to keep some things quiet?"

"Not when you have something amazing and important together. Why wouldn't you be open about it?"

"I don't know, Soph. Two people could have strong feelings for each other but still have reasons to keep it private. Take Romeo and Juliet."

I don't agree with her, but this is a writing workshop, not a personal philosophy class. We move on to some of my earlier poems, so she can see how my work has progressed during the week. I show her my first poem here, with the Shakespearean rhyme scheme, and tell her how I was able to free myself to the more complicated Petrarchan and Spenserian structures.

"They still seem pretty structured to me."

"You're missing the point! I love the structures and I want to be able to work within them. They have a rich history and are worth bringing into the twenty-first century." I can't tell if she doesn't like the structures or if she thinks I shouldn't be fitting my work into them.

I'm relieved when Joan comes by to speak with both of us.

"Soph, you've done a big part of what you came here to do. But now I'd like to see you take the next step, push beyond your goal, and take your work up a level."

"What do you mean?"

"I mean that, having gotten to the more complicated forms, you should try something you didn't set out to do, something more than your goal."

"Like what?"

"That's not for me to say, Soph." She smiles. "I'm confident you can figure it out. Poetry has structure, style, content, and emotion. What would you like to expand in yours?"

I'm frowning as she turns back to Gabriela.

Tess.

THEY PAIR ME WITH ORLY for peer review.

Orly and I both take our writing samples into the lounge, but some of the other girls are there and I ask her if she wants to come up to our room where it's quiet.

She hesitates, then asks, "Are you sure?" I can hear a little tremor in her voice, as though she's nervous. I nod and smile, and we walk up the stairs.

Orly sits on Soph's bed, and I sit on mine. We agree to spend a half hour reading each other's work. The chapter I have is about Orly's memory of a summer day.

> *Lawrence Irwin drowned right in front of me the summer I turned five. I don't remember it. My ten-year-old sister Rose was supposed to be watching me. By her account, she went to the snack bar, fixing to buy us a popsicle with the dollar bill Mama gave her, when she heard the ruckus, all whistles and screaming. Four lifeguards leapt from their high chairs and dove into the deep end of the pool.*
>
> *Rose says I was still whining for the popsicle as she stood by the pool, terrified and mesmerized by little Lawrence under the water in his star-spangled trunks, his face tinged blue.*
>
> *We went to the pool most days of that hotter-than-blazes summer. Mama, Daddy, and Meemaw worked all day, and the pool was where all the kids in town went. A few of the stay-at-home moms were officially in charge, rubbing on sunscreen*

and handing out Band-Aids to their own kids and any others who landed in front of them. No one really thought about whether it was safe. Of course it was safe; it was Allenton, Georgia. We had two stoplights, a Pepsi factory, and a pine mill out by the used-car dealer on Route 17.

I don't remember Lawrence or the lifeguards or everyone getting out of the pool at once. I wasn't there, in the back office of the changing house, when the manager, poor Mrs. Bowen, surrounded by paramedics, pulled out the alphabetical membership list to call Lawrence's mother and let her know what had happened. Our names were so similar, and Mrs. Bowen was so shaken, anyone could understand why her finger landed like a bug on "Erwin" and she never reached the Irwins.

Mama got the call at her desk in the reception area of the local community college. She said later that she could barely hear Mrs. Bowen whispering into the phone. But Mama heard the word "drowned" and she flew out the door without her purse, not even telling her boss she was leaving.

I don't remember Lawrence, but I will never forget Mama's arrival that day. She pushed her way through the crowd of adults and children near the empty pool. First she grabbed Rose, but when she saw me fussing and grabbing for the forgotten popsicle in Rose's hand, now gone to a sticky, orange mess, Mama hollered. I froze, terrified. She grabbed me hard and held me for several long minutes while she wept. I squirmed in embarrassment and Rose petted her shoulder, both of us still in the dark about why she flew off the handle like that.

"I've got you, baby," she told me over and over. "I've got you always."

Soph thinks I have it hard, but reading this piece makes being who I am feel pretty simple, even if parts of it are still not easy. I tell Orly I'm glad she wrote it, because I've never met a transgender person and maybe lots of people who never have either will read her story and learn about her life. But I've also never met anyone from Georgia and that part is interesting too. She writes in a way that makes it sound like its own planet, not just another state in the same country as New Hampshire. It makes me wish Chris would read it.

After she finishes reading I say, "Can I ask you a personal question?" I'm not sure how she's going to react.

"I can guess. You want to know when I first figured out I was a girl."

"No."

"Really? That's usually what people ask."

"I was just wondering what made you decide to tell."

Orly looks at me as though she's trying to figure something out, and I can feel my face turn red. I shouldn't be asking her these kinds of questions. But she says, "I was little. It wasn't a question of telling. I acted the way my sister acted. And when my parents tried to treat me like a boy, I just knew I had to correct them. I never thought about keeping quiet."

She stands up then, stares out the window, and says, "And now, anyone who didn't know me then doesn't ask. I like that."

"Not having to explain yourself all the time?"

"Yeah."

"I'm sorry," I say. She shrugs, but she doesn't look mad. I'm not sure what else to say.

After Orly leaves, I go upstairs to grab a computer to work on my final chapter. I know how the story is going to end. It's funny how making that decision to write the characters doing something *out of character* actually made me figure out how to write this story differently. Maybe this conference has taught me something.

But as I'm headed down the third-floor hall, I spy Chris in her room through her door, which is open a little. Before I know what I'm doing, I'm knocking on it.

✳   ✳   ✳

From Soph Alcazar's Writing Journal,
February 16, 2018

Am I allowed to be feeling this hurt?
Heartsick, I want to proclaim, to assert.

Chapter Twenty-Four

From the Fan Fiction Unbound Archive,
posted by conTessaofthecastle:

Daphne breathed in the scent of roses and ash so familiar to her. She didn't want to move, for fear it would disappear again. "I don't understand," Daphne murmured. Astoria was real, was here, wasn't gone forever. "I never found the spell-caster. How did I make it happen?"

Soph.

AFTER THE PEER REVIEW, I'M not sure what to do with myself, so I go back to our room. I want to try to talk to Tess again, to convince her to come out here, even if it's only for a day. She's in our room. But she isn't alone. It's dark, and I step in and turn on the lamp next to my bed, figuring Tess doesn't want to talk to me and I should get my book and go. To my surprise, Chris is sitting there. They look up at me.

"Hey," says Chris. She sounds nervous.

"Soph, Chris and I were talking." Tess continues to surprise me. Here she is, reserved and refusing to put herself out there all day after opening up to me last night. Then she goes and *still* tries to figure out someone like Chris.

"Do you want me to leave?" Chris and I both say it at the same time and, since neither of us knows how to answer, we turn to Tess.

"This is Soph's room, too," Tess says, glancing at me, and I remember last night. "Do you mind if she stays?" she asks. Chris shrugs. Tess walks over to her bed. "We talked the other night over here," she says, pointing to my bed. "Let's move. We don't have any more chairs." She sits down and pushes herself sideways across the bed until she's up against the wall. I sit next to her and Chris sits on her other side, exactly as we were during the power outage, only on Tess's bed.

"No Hennessy today," teases Tess. That breaks the ice. I roll my eyes and snort.

Chris giggles and says, "Never again."

I smile, and we relax.

Tess breaks the silence. "Chris was telling me about what happened with Orly. I told her I wanted to know. The same way she wanted to know about her old boyfriend." Tess turns in my direction and adds, "I don't think Soph is going to be critical. And we can agree to keep it to ourselves if you want. Soph can keep a secret."

Hearing that makes me want to scream with equal measures of joy and frustration. Tess trusts me, so maybe last night was not a one-time thing. But she's also telling me to keep my mouth shut about it, which kills me. I can do that. At least, I can do that until the two of us are alone.

I say, "Yeah, Chris. I would like to know. I promise not to get pissed." I want to push my thigh close to Tess, to be able to feel her next to me, but I'm not sure how she will react. Instead I push away from her a few inches. She notices.

Chris's face softens as she talks. "I wanted to come to a writing workshop to do some work I could use for colleges and to try to publish an article. I didn't know all this was going to happen." She puts her head down, shaking it.

Tess lets the silence hang, then asks quietly, "What happened with Orly?"

Chris fiddles with the bottom button on her sweater. "They sent me her name. His name. I don't know how to say it. Nothing other than his name."

I'm about to correct her again when I feel Tess's hand, like a warning, on my arm. I hold my tongue.

"No one said anything about trans girls. Or what that means. Or gave me any warning at all. Then Orly shows up the first night, and there's all this weirdness about changing clothes, and I figure out that she isn't really a girl. Or that she's a girl with boy parts. Like I said, I don't know how to say it." She stares at Soph. "Maybe this happens all the time in New York. I don't know. I never met a trans person."

I'm probably not supposed to break in, but I can't help myself. "Chris, what does it matter that you never met a trans girl? I've never met anyone from Dallas. So what?"

She's getting frustrated.

"I didn't think I was going to be put in a room with a guy without being told."

"Orly's not a guy, and why are you worried about boys? They're just boys."

"The point is, I didn't know! What I *did* know is that I got a roommate who's a stranger to me and has a—" She stumbles over the word, then says, "A *thing*. That's a lot different from being put in a room with a girl you don't know from Atlanta. If my parents knew about that, they'd never have let me come. And then when I figured out some more stuff about it, it was too late to go talk to Professor Forsythe, because everyone got mad at me—even Yin—all because of a dumb joke that Orly didn't even care about."

I'm not sure what she is trying to say, so I ask, "What did you figure out?""

Chris stares at the ceiling. I can't see her that well on the other side of Tess, but I can tell she's thinking about what words to use.

She sighs and says, "I researched trans kids."

Well, that *is* news.

Tess asks quietly, "What did you find out?"

Chris explains that she first found all the statistics about trans kids and how they have lots of safety concerns. "Then I went and tracked down the rules for various school districts about overnight trips and it turns out lots of them say you can't tell someone like me about their roommate being trans. It's like not allowing someone to opt out of having a Black roommate or a Muslim roommate. It would be considered prejudice." She sighs and shakes her head. "Then Grace gave me a lecture yesterday. She told me I was wrong, and that the professors found out about the carrot thing. Now I'm all confused about everything. I just want to go home."

"Chris, you say you're interested in journalism. I know you're good at it because of the investigation you did for our Maizy Donovan piece."

Huh? The last I heard, Chris wasn't involved. But Tess keeps talking without explaining.

"What if you talk to Orly? She might have told the instructors or she might have had a reason not to." Chris doesn't say anything, so Tess continues. "Wouldn't you rather try to get to know her instead of leaving tomorrow knowing you didn't ask?"

Tess picks up her phone as if she's going to text Orly and invite her over, but I tell her I'll go myself. I'd rather let Orly know what's going on ahead of time.

Orly answers her door holding a book in one hand. She has on that oversized sweater she was wearing the first day. She is not interested in coming to see Chris.

"Why would I?" she asks. I don't have a good answer, except that Tess asked me to ask her. I tell her that and she cocks her head as if I said something important. She puts down her book and follows me back to our room.

The lights are all on in our room now, and the sky is darker outside. Tess is showing Chris something on her phone and asking her questions. You would think they were friends, like they'd been friends all week.

Tess greets Orly with a smile and pushes over on the bed to make room for her. Chris doesn't say anything.

Orly doesn't sit on the bed. "Well, I'm here."

No one says anything. I guess we are each expecting someone else to go first. Tess wades in. "Orly, Chris says that she was surprised when she met you. Surprised and a little frightened. Right, Chris?" Chris nods slightly. "But we thought maybe if we all talked, we could clear this up. We're going home tomorrow. It would be nice if we could work this out first."

Orly is silent. Then she sighs and says, "I just wanted to get along."

Chris sits up. "I don't want to know your private life. But I do want to know who I'm rooming with." She juts out her chin. "You acted like it was a joke anyway, Orly. Besides, I already apologized. Why can't you just drop it?"

Orly shakes her head and says very quietly, "You need to be honest. You didn't feel unsafe, and you didn't mean it as a joke. Believe me, just because I wasn't intimidated doesn't mean I thought it was a joke. I reckon you know that."

I'm about to back her up when I feel Tess's hand on my arm. I hold my tongue.

"You did it to try and make every other girl uncomfortable with me." Orly continues. "And you only apologized to me after Grace made you."

Chris protests. "Look, I wanted a story. I admit that. But I apologized, and it's still not good enough."

"Of course it's not good enough!" Orly raises her voice. "You just don't want to be in trouble anymore."

"No, no. I did some research and I understand much more about trans kids—"

Orly cuts her off. "Let me tell you something, Chris, you don't get to tell anyone else how to walk into a room. *I* get to decide whether to tell people about myself and *I* get to decide when I want to do that, whether it's where I'm from, what kind of girl I am, or anything else. If you want to call yourself a feminist, you need to let me make those choices myself."

Chris ducks her head. "I think we're just really different people. I don't know how you change that."

Orly says, "You change that by educating yourself. We're not that different. We're both Southern girls who want to be writers."

Chris furrows her forehead. Orly looks at the ceiling, composing herself. She catches my eye, then continues. "I'm not a threat to you, Chris, and you thinking I am is *your* problem, not mine."

I think Chris is about to leave, with everyone still upset, when Tess pulls printed pages out of her knapsack. She shows them to Orly and asks if she can read them. Orly shrugs and glances at Chris. I'm not sure what Tess is doing until she reads part of Orly's memoir out loud.

> *It's cold on Christmas morning, the year I turn ten. I can see my breath when I open the front door to let Hallie the dachshund out for her walk. My feet are cold when I step barefoot onto the concrete stoop to call her back in. The morning is waking up, winter sun struggling to climb in the sky. Inside, Mama fusses with coffee and homemade coffeecake even though no one wants to eat anything when the tree is surrounded by packages. Then there will be church, followed by turkey and ham for Christmas dinner at Meemaw's. Uncle Howard will play Christmas carols at the old piano, and Aunt Gwen will tell me to stand up straight and stop fidgeting. It's the same every year, and that's what I like best about it.*

Tess stops reading. "It sounds like Christmas in my house," she says, "except there's no way I could go out barefoot, obviously. And we have a collie named Felix, not a dachshund."

"We have a poodle," says Chris quietly. She looks quickly at Orly. "Named Bella."

"I don't have a dog," I say, "but my Aunt Valentina is always telling me to stand up straight on holidays. What is *that* about?"

We sit around talking and showing each other pictures on our phones until it gets darker outside and a little less awkward in our room.

Tess.

THE CONFERENCE SCHEDULE SAID THERE would be a formal farewell banquet on Saturday night. I brought one of my church dresses to wear, because I don't have anything else. I knew it would be wrong when I packed it, but it feels even more wrong now.

Chris and Orly have gone back to their rooms to change. I don't know if I handled that right, but I still feel bad that I didn't speak up for Orly when Chris first talked to me. I've pretty much given up on finding some way to be a leader here. Maybe I should just cancel the interview next week. There doesn't seem to be much point.

Soph, in one of her lacy black bras and matching black underwear, is pulling clothes out of her duffel bag and flinging them all over the bed. I see a black leather miniskirt, a sheer black blouse, and a gold tank top. Little high-heeled, open-toed suede booties land on the floor. Things are still tense between us since breakfast, and even though she isn't giving me the silent treatment, she's kept her distance during the day's activities. Even now, after what we did with Chris and Orly, she's pretty quiet.

I messed this whole thing up and I have no idea how to fix it. I also have no idea how to stop staring at Soph in her underwear, until she looks up at me and that does the trick. I instantly look away. I stare at my light pink shift dress, plain navy flats, and navy cardigan sweater. I don't know who I am or who I want to be anymore. Soph looks at the pile of clothes on her bed and then back at me. I'm still wearing the black sweater she loaned me this morning.

"Do you want to borrow something?" she asks with a little smile, like a peace offering. She gives me a couple of outfits to try on, but the skirts are too tiny, and they're all wrong with my shoes anyway. Finally, I put on my own dress, and Soph wraps a thick leather belt with a double-row of metal grommets around my waist. Then she snaps a leather cuff with more metal on it around my wrist. She has fishnet tights in her bag, which I put on, and by the time she's finished changing my outfit, I don't look at all as though I'm going to Our Lady of Mercy.

"I love dressing up," she says as she adjusts my dress for a little too long. "I wish you could come to one of my school dances."

Soph texts Orly to come and do my makeup. Orly gives me smoky eyes. Then she pulls my hair off my face with a huge silver metal clip and puts this dark fuchsia lipstick on me, which is more than amazing. Orly also gives me some dangly silver earrings and makes me take off my Pandora bracelet. I've never worn this much metal or this much makeup, but it feels more like me than I think I probably have ever felt. It's funny how wearing Soph's things makes me feel that way.

By the time Soph is dressed in her own black and gold outfit and Orly has given her the reddest lips I've ever seen outside of a movie, we're all laughing and the tension has dissipated. Orly is wearing a flouncy skirt and a simple black top with an infinity scarf and more dangly earrings. Soph makes us take pictures all squeezed together. I even take some on my phone and send one to Joey.

The three of us go down to dinner, and Soph surprises me. She sits right next to me, and though she doesn't look at me while she's talking to Orly and Clover, under the tablecloth she holds my hand for the entire meal.

After dinner, Professor Forsythe stands and announces that she has selected one of the group projects for a reading. "I think you'll enjoy it as much as I did, for its entertainment value, its cleverness, and the spirited message it delivers."

Soph's group reads its project. She didn't tell me. Each girl tells parts of the story, in song, verse, free verse, and as a blog. Freya has a husband and a wife; the husband's feelings are hurt, and Freya uses magical implements to find him. She wants him back and is about to use a magic necklace when they discover that they all like each other and it works out. Each of the girls in the group hams up her own part, and we're all laughing when Soph steps forward to give the conclusion in one of her complicated sonnets.

Thus did Freya find Od to bring him in.
And just as the two of them did marry,
Freya found Stola and love nonpareil,
Love without need for the Brísingamen.

Od, devastated, did flee the women,
Believe his love a corpse to bury.
Only then did Freya react and query.
She loved both lady and gentleman.

Freya believed only charms could mend,
Her bond with Od her new love caused to rend,
Found Od, and prepared a magic amend.
But Stola and Od, quick to each other befriend
Added their own love, the marriage to extend.
The moral is three as well as two can blend.

When they finish, Soph smiles at me, and I smile back, clapping as hard as I can.

❊　❊　❊

LATER THAT NIGHT, BACK IN our room, Soph closes the door and leaves the lights off. I reach for her tentatively. She pulls me into a hug. She kisses me, and I kiss her back. Everything outside this room is complicated, but here I can breathe. I never want to leave this room ever again.

As we're getting undressed, I hand Soph her belt and I sit on the bed to strip off the fishnet tights. I leave the leather wrist cuff on. I'm thinking about leaving tomorrow, and I ask Soph, "What should I tell Joey about us?"

She turns toward me, startled, then sits down on her bed across from me. She has already taken off her skirt and her tights and is now pulling off the shimmery blouse she had on at dinner. I can barely see her.

"I don't know, Tess. What do you want to tell him?"

"Can we…" I want to talk to her more about this, but mostly I want to touch her skin while we talk, and I don't know how to ask her for that. I can feel my face heating up.

Soph must sense it because she says, "Let's get under the covers and talk." I'm relieved that she didn't make me ask out loud.

After we've undressed and washed off the lipstick and the eyeshadow, we climb together into my bed. With the door locked and the lights out, I curl into Soph and close my eyes. She's warm and comforting. The darkness makes it easier to say what I'm thinking.

"I never lie to Joey. I don't want to lie to him about meeting you. Or about how much you mean to me."

"Okay." I can hear the question in Soph's tone. She doesn't ask it though.

"I don't…" I feel selfish, but I also need to tell Soph. She deserves to know, even if it makes her mad.

"I don't know how I'm supposed to have a boyfriend, you know, a boyfriend in the sense that we have, when there's you… and I don't know how not to either."

"Okay," she says again, but now I can't read her tone. I guess there's nothing I can do to keep her from getting mad again. I need to be clear about this. I say it all in a rush.

"I need to keep being there for him until we graduate. Even though I want… I want to see you again. I—can't break up with him. Not now." My voice cracks a little when I say it.

I'm sure she's going to climb out of bed now and leave me alone. Then she'll lecture me about how I need to come out to everyone in Castleton and I'm not being fair to her. I brace myself for it. In fact, I push back from her side a little, to give her the room to leave, though I'm sure I will shatter into a million little pieces when she does.

But instead she pulls me back toward her and puts her hand in my hair, stroking it gently. She says, "You never want to see anyone left out, do you, Tess?"

That surprises me. I've never thought about it like that. She keeps talking, her voice low, her hand still on my hair. "All week, you kept trying to convince Chris to work with you, to make sure Orly wasn't left out without making the other girls mad. Then you were the one who said we had to go find Chris when she was missing. No one else wanted to do that."

"You went with me," I say, a little embarrassed now. I feel her shrug next to me.

"I went for the Hennessy." That makes me laugh.

"I think things work better when everyone is part of the group. I don't always feel as though I fit in and I guess it means something to me to try to make sure other people do too. Just like I can't leave Joey on his own, not now. He doesn't have any other friends he can talk to about stuff. Not in Castleton."

Soph makes a humming noise, as though she's thinking about something, and then simply says, "All right."

Once I've figured out she isn't leaving and settle back against her, she tells me that I can be like Freya, the Norse goddess of love and war, who has both a man and a woman in her life, and they all care about each other in different ways. That turns into more kissing.

✳ ✳ ✳

From Soph Alcazar's Writing Journal,
February 16, 2018

I want her to come out, culpa mea,
But I can be Stola to her Freya.

Chapter Twenty-Five

From the Fan Fiction Unbound Archive,
posted by conTessaofthecastle:

A woman came in from the other room, startling Daphne, who reached for Astoria, prepared to utter the shape-shifting spell again.

Astoria spoke in her ear. "You shifted me to her when you said the spell in the forest."

Daphne peered up at a wrinkled face, a kind smile, and a hand holding out the mug of tea Astoria had set down.

"You've had a long journey," said the spell-caster.

Soph.

I WAKE UP BEFORE TESS. There's so much I want to ask her, I'm almost buzzing with anticipation, pressed up against her back. But it feels so good lying close to her while she sleeps that I try not to move. I never thought about this part before, what it would be like waking up next to someone you don't want to be apart from. She wakes up slowly, something I didn't expect from her. I'm lying on my side with my arm over her waist.

"You're up with the cows," she jokes. She turns on her back, her right side up against me.

"Tess," I ask, "why did you keep trying to bring Chris into the fold?"

"Interesting phrase, Soph." She yawns and ducks her head closer to me. "Do you know what 'the fold' is?"

I've heard the phrase, but I don't know what it really means. She continues.

"A 'fold' is a fenced-in area, like a paddock. You bring the herd or the flock in so that they are safe and together."

I chuckle. "So, you were trying to bring Chris safely into the fold on Thursday night when the power went out. Only that's not exactly what I meant. You said then that you weren't supposed to leave a soldier on the field. But you went further than that. Even though she was horrible to Orly and wouldn't cooperate with your group, you offered to teach her to skate. You invited her to go sledding with us. A few days ago, I thought you were going to shove that carrot up her nose. Then, yesterday, you had her in here and got her to make up with Orly."

"Soph, a baby calf was born at home right before I came here."

Tess tells me about struggling with the mother to get her to nurse her baby, and how she left the calf too long and it got kicked into a corner of the barn.

"Putting feed on Angie, that should have attracted her mother. We had to try something else. And then, when her mother still wouldn't learn, we had to take care of Angie a different way."

I don't get it.

"Soph, even if Angie lives, she won't be as strong as the rest. The herd might not accept her. I don't know if her mother really hurt her when she kicked her away, and that's on me. I shouldn't have left her alone. I didn't do the job Daddy trusted me to do. She could still die."

I still don't understand. "But, I mean, Angie's mother is supposed to feed her own baby, right? You shouldn't have to do that in the first place."

"In a way, yes. But Angie's mother *didn't* do it. We can't let a cow die if we can save it. They're worth money, but they're also… I don't know exactly how to explain this, but calves are part of the farm. They're *ours*, not just their mothers'. So it *is* my responsibility. Mine and Daddy's and Molly's and Mom's. And we have to keep trying with the mother, even when she's wrong and stubborn about being wrong. The same way, even though Daddy was mad at me, he still gave me another chance to get it right."

Tess.

SOPH LETS GO OF ME and rolls onto her back. She stares at the ceiling. "Tess, you're going to make a great cadet."

I shake my head. "I doubt I'll be admitted."

"Why?"

I remind her. "I've got my interview next week with the admissions panel. I still don't have a good answer for that leadership question. That's enough for them to reject me." I don't want to admit, even to Soph, even now, here, how much I want to get in.

She sits up suddenly. Cold air hits me when she pushes back the covers. "Come on, Tess, you must see it!"

"What do you mean?"

"I mean what you just told me, what you did here with Chris. How can you not see this?"

"No, you don't understand, Soph. It's not about just doing the right thing." She makes a face. "I didn't take everyone here and save them or anything."

"I think *you* don't understand, Tess." She puts her hand in mine, still tangled in the blankets. Her palm is warm. "You stood up in front of everyone and confronted Chris. Then, when no one else thought about it, you went to make sure Chris was safe. When we found her, you insisted on making her stay with us."

"I don't think that's quite what West Point has in mind, Soph. All I was trying to do was understand both sides and not leave anyone out. Besides, it's not like Chris and Orly ended up friends."

"I'm not even finished. You were like a general or something, mediating differences between Chris and Orly. We learned in American History about how Eisenhower did that when he took command in World War II. You got Chris to speak directly to Orly when no one else would because you kept trying to understand. Maybe Chris and Orly *didn't* end up being friends. But *you* and Orly did."

I'm quiet for a few moments. Then I sigh. "I need to think about it. It doesn't sound like a very traditional answer."

"Oh, god, tradition. You had to say that word?" She must be thinking about her mother, because she flings herself down next to me again, still holding my hand. I smile at the drama.

"Soph, you're more of a traditionalist than you think."

"I'm not!" she insists.

"What's your big passion, Soph? I mean besides social justice, coming out, and texting?"

I smile to show her that I'm kidding. Her face is close to mine, and she smiles too. "Writing, I guess."

"Yuh, writing. What kinds of poems?"

"Oh. Sonnets. Okay. Sonnets from the thirteenth to the sixteenth centuries. But I don't use the same language or the same topics."

"No, you don't. You take the tradition and you adapt it. But that's part of what traditions are, right? Like Orly's piece about Christmas. Every family does it a little differently, but the part everyone understands is how people look forward to it every year in the same way."

"Tess." She looks at me seriously. "You also showed great leadership when you kissed me first."

"Shut. Up." I say, as I push a pillow at her face until she pushes back and laughs that glittery laugh.

⁕ ⁕ ⁕

From Soph Alcazar's Writing Journal,
February 17, 2018

I know I can't give her a directive.
She shows me the value of collective.

Chapter Twenty-Six

From the Fan Fiction Unbound Archive,
posted by conTessaofthecastle:

Daphne drank the warm liquid gratefully, tucked into the safe embrace of Astoria's arms. The spell-caster moved quietly around the room, placing plates of food on the table by the fire. She didn't seem surprised by Daphne's presence. When the tea was gone, Daphne set the mug down carefully and said, "I still don't understand. How did I make it happen?"

Soph.

AT BREAKFAST, EVERYONE IS BUZZING about our final readings. I sit with Tess and hold her hand under the table, but I'm distracted by what she said earlier. I'm still worried about my own reading. Joan and Grace didn't seem too impressed and neither did Yin or Gabriela. Yesterday, I thought I had pretty much accomplished what I wanted to do here, being able to work in the more complicated sonnet forms. Now I can't help but wonder if I've done enough.

While we're finishing, Professor Forsythe tells us that the bus is waiting to take us to Minerva College for the tour. I've been waiting for this visit all week. Except... I let go of Tess's hand

and she turns to me, a question on her face. I tell her something has come up.

I clear my place setting. Once I've put my dishes in the kitchen, I approach Professor Forsythe. "Professor, I was wondering if I could stay here while everyone else is visiting Minerva. I'd like to work on my final piece for this afternoon."

While everyone is away, I think about what I want to do. So far, I've done Shakespearean, Petrarchan, and Spenserian. But being with Tess makes me think that the structures don't have to be stiff. Or maybe I don't have to keep within the confines I thought I did.

I write for three hours. I'm so absorbed that I'm surprised when I hear the bus pulling up out front. I have two poems on my screen. I need to make a choice.

⁕ ⁕ ⁕

WHEN WE'RE ALL ASSEMBLED IN the lounge, I volunteer to go first. Professor Forsythe nods at me and I stand.

"The point of a sonnet is to propose a situation with an argument and come to a conclusion or resolution. But poets do it in strict formats. I came here writing couplets and hoped to be able to expand into the true classical forms of Petrarch, Spenser, and Shakespeare. I did that. In fact, I had a Shakespearian sonnet I was prepared to read this afternoon. But I think I learned something about structure and myself and tradition this week. Maybe in more ways than one." I can't help looking at Tess. Her eyes widen.

"I decided that maybe I was sticking to the traditional forms too much. I like those structures and the idea that they work in different languages and times. But Petrarch gave way to Shakespeare, Shakespeare to Spenser, and there are other variations. I said at the very first group discussion that culture has continually reworked prior content. We've called it legend, myth, satire, homage, and fan fiction. Now it's my turn to create a structure."

"My *Sophronian* sonnet has its own rhyme scheme and its own meter. The structure is ABC CBA BAC CAB DD. Rather than even numbered sections, I have three-line stanzas. The lines are of different lengths. A is ten syllables, B is eight, C is six and D reverts to the full ten. Here is 'My Time at the Conference.'"

I, sure of myself in January,
Knew just what I wanted and sought.
Naive was I, a kid.

I came here, made my bid.
Structure informed by just my thoughts.
Why couldn't it work in February?

I surely knew how people ought
To comport and treat each other fairly.
And here, that's what I did.

I was, it seems, rigid.
To apply rules, I should have been wary.
A broader view to me you taught.

The most significant of tradition
Survives and blooms through endless revision.

Tess.

SOPH LOOKS TENTATIVELY PLEASED WITH herself when she finishes. I wish I could give her a hug. I settle for grinning at her as broadly as I can. We make eye contact, and she flushes.

Professor Forsythe nods approvingly. "Soph has very creatively fused old and new, something the four of us hoped she would try. She may now join the twentieth-century poets Lowell, Heaney, and others in showing the elasticity of the form." She nods to Grace, Joan, and Celestine, who smile at Soph. "Soph was paired with Gabriela and I'd like to hear what Gabriela thinks about the final product." Gabriela says something, but I'm only half listening. I can feel my stomach churn, since I still need to read my final chapter.

While Clover is reading her work, Soph passes me a piece of paper folded in quarters. We can't talk but she makes a face as though she wants me to read it. I open the page slowly, trying not to make any noise, and read.

I prided myself on thinking I knew
Why to come out and avoid any blow.
I studied and read and learned to be true.
Nobody should have to remain down low.

Cold winter snow invades my empty heart,
But she could be here, her hand extending.

Will shame and closet doors keep us apart?
Can I penetrate what she's defending?

In a crucible of ice, snowsister
Defiled, I question what safety may be.
She confronts; I'm surprised; Then kissed by her
Before understanding her own safety.

Now I can see. My world view is reformed.
She schooled me. The kiss, pink night: my heart warmed.

Soph waits until I'm finished. When I turn back to her, she quietly takes the paper from my hand, folds it up and tucks it into the back pocket of my jeans. She says, "It's Shakespearian, not Sophronian, but I thought it fit."

Soph.

I PEEK BRIEFLY AT HER, hoping she's not mad. She's pink. I don't mean her pink clothing; I mean her face is pink, but not as if she's embarrassed or angry. She's glowing, though she looks away when she sees me looking at her. Her eyes are wide, and she has a little smile on her face. I want to grab her and dance with her right here in this room in the middle of everyone. But of course, I don't. Not doing something I want to on the spur of the moment is harder than I thought it would be.

I don't listen to most of the other readings. I can't get a feel for them if they're part of a longer piece. I do listen to Orly's, though. I'm pretty impressed that someone our age can write a memoir so powerful.

Tess.

THE NEXT ONE TO READ is Chris. Everyone in the room must be nervous, including Chris. But she reads a piece about how our group went from being strangers to everyone being nervous around each other because of their differences to people allowing each other to be who they are, including herself, and she acknowledges everyone's courage in stepping out of their comfort zones. She avoids the word "safe," but I can't blame her.

Then it's my turn. When Orly talks about my work, she says she likes how I took the two witches, Daphne and Astoria, and made them completely different from how they were in the show, but in a way that is true to their personalities. She mentions that she went online last night to check out the rest of my story, and found out that I had close to thirty-three thousand hits on it. Most of the girls look impressed. Under her breath, Yin says "Wow."

When Orly says, "Tess made me believe that two women together could create their own magic, even when they are fighting against the rest of the world," I dare to look in Soph's direction, and she's smiling at me. So I take a deep breath, and I read the ending out loud, to the whole room.

Astoria pulled Daphne into her arms and embraced her firmly. Daphne could feel Astoria's hands splayed across her back, each finger a small pressure point of love. Astoria whispered into her ear, "From this day onward, we'll always move as one." Daphne couldn't stop the tears from forming in her eyes, couldn't stop herself from breathing in the heady scent of roses and ash that had become the smell of home to her, couldn't stop herself from kissing Astoria, tenderly but a little bit fiercely.

Soph.

SHE LOOKS UP AT ME when she's finished—not at anyone else, but at me. I'm shocked all over again, and I can tell from her expression that she's nervous. I clap and I do it loudly enough that everyone has to join in. I think to myself that she's an incredibly strong person, strong enough to keep it in while she needs to and strong enough to break free when she can.

Tess.

THE CONFERENCE IS ALMOST OVER. Professor Forsythe tells us how impressed she and Joan, Celestine, and Grace are and says that they will stay in touch with us for as long as we want. We can contact them by email and we should tell the Austen-Browning Institute where we go to college and when we publish our work— Professor Forsythe says she's sure we will.

Then she surprises everybody by making a speech:

"We need to talk about something important, about safety. The Institute picked the twenty-four of you based on two factors. First, the quality of your written work. Second, that you are young women." She pauses. "We are aware that there was an issue this week because you have physical differences."

No one says anything.

Professor Forsythe continues. "Oh, my friends, I can tell you from a long career, that as women you will be subject to unfair judgments based on your bodies. Those judgments are hard on the psyche. They distract us from what we want to do. They demean our work by promoting the irrelevant. I urge you to refrain from judging each other. As you go out into the world, you will face real attacks on your safety. Please don't add to the attacks on your own friends and colleagues. Support your differences and accept them. Celebrate them. Hold on to each other. Find ways to build trust with one another. Women need each other's support. You may not understand that now, but I promise one day you will."

"Now, before we break, we have a few minutes to exchange contact information and bid farewell to each other. We'll be circulating and hope to speak with each of you before you leave. Help yourself to coffee, tea, and cookies."

We have an hour to pack, but I'm finished really quickly. Soph is downstairs looking for her laptop charger, so I sit on my bed for the last time and pull out a spiral notebook. I have a few things I want to write down before I go back to Castleton. The words I haven't found in all this time come quickly. I look at the last paragraph.

> *I'm not sure I understand everything about leadership, but I learned this in Granite Notch: I can change how I treat other people, even if I can't change how they treat me. I can take what I know, and then learn about what I don't. I can listen. I can apologize and I can attempt to walk in someone else's shoes. I can try different things and see what works, and*

I can ask for help understanding. Sometimes people will let me down. I just don't want to be one of those people.

I find Orly and hug her goodbye. She invites me to stay with her in Atlanta anytime. Gabriela finds me and asks for my fan fiction name so she can follow me. I'm putting her email into my phone when Professor Forsythe goes up to Soph. She's smiling.

"You read some very impressive poetry earlier, Soph. You made the creative leap we hope the best of our attendees will make. I'm glad you took the extra time you needed to focus on what was most important this week. I hope to hear from you."

Soph is speechless, which I'm guessing doesn't happen often. But then she grins like a little kid and says, "Oh. You will. I mean, thank you. Thank you."

Chapter Twenty-Seven

From the Fan Fiction Unbound Archive,
posted by conTessaofthecastle:

"We made it happen together," said Astoria simply.

Soph.

I KNOW TESS HAS TO go home and she can't tell her family about us. But her family didn't keep her from standing up for Orly and it didn't keep her from kissing me. I'm *so* glad it didn't keep her from kissing me.

Tess and I go back to our room to pack. When we close the door, I say, "I know I didn't understand it before, Tess. But I think I do now, and I hope—"

She cuts me off. "No, Soph, no. I… well, I know it all from your sonnet '"My world view is reformed.'" I smile at her. She continues, "So is mine. And telling people like that, through my writing, it scares me, but it's exciting. Like meeting you."

We're quiet then, until I reach out a hand to her and she comes close to me. We hold each other, standing up first, then lying on my bed. But we don't have much time. The shuttle bus to the airport gets here in half an hour, so we separate and pack. I can't help but ask, "Can I text you? After we go home?"

Tess nods and smiles. "Yeah. Definitely. My parents don't read that stuff. Joey and I text all the time."

I gulp to suppress a sob. It makes me happy knowing we'll stay connected. "And we'll see each other again. I want it so much that I know I can make it happen."

She chuckles indulgently, as my father would. "I bet you can, Soph. Although why a city girl like you wants to come to Minerva College for four years still is a mystery to me."

I pull the black sweater she wore yesterday out of my bag and hold it out to her. She puts it in the bottom of her bag without saying a word. "I still have your socks, you know," I remind her. "Could I take them home as a trade?"

She nods, smiling. A question passes across her face, but she hesitates.

"What, Tess?"

"Soph, would you read my leadership thing?"

"Sure, but isn't it for an interview?"

"I know, but I wanted to write it down first, so I don't choke when it comes up." She hands me a piece of notebook paper.

She looks really nervous when I finish my reading. I say, "You nailed it," and I get to hug her again.

Tess's cell phone rings.

"Oh, hi, yes. I'll be down in a minute." She looks at me. "I want you to meet Joey, if you will. He wants to meet you too."

It's as if I'm being introduced to family. My chest feels full, but Tess is waiting for me to answer her. So I pull myself together and say, "Yeah, definitely. Let me zip up my Vera… my duffel."

There's no missing Joey. He's in a big light blue truck. The truck is old, like something a tough guy would drive on TV.

Tess goes to the driver's side and asks him to get out. He doesn't look like the gay guys I know. He's big. Not tall, but big. I don't mean fat. He has a big head of shaggy blonde hair, and the hand he holds out when Tess introduces us is gigantic. He's friendly, though, and when he smiles at me I'm surprised that I feel suddenly shy.

"You must be the roommate." I notice his jaw is lopsided, and he talks out of one side of his mouth. I look down in case he's self-conscious.

"Nice to meet you, Joey." I can't think of anything else to say. I don't have any idea what Tess might have told him or what is still a secret.

Tess stands next to me and puts an arm around my waist. "We're due back before evening milking."

Joey looks at me as if he already knows me. He nods and says, "Nice to meet you too, Soph. In person. I'm glad you had a good week."

I turn to Tess, careful not to dislodge the arm which feels so good right above my hip. I don't want to embarrass her, so I roll into her and put my head next to hers. I say into her ear, up close, "Tess, I don't want my last kiss from you. Not yet." I feel her squeeze me and nod.

"So, this won't be the last one," she says and kisses me, right there, in front of Joey and the lodge. She recites my own words back to me before she leaves, "'She could be here, her hand extending.'"

I feel a vibration and think at first that my heart might be exploding, but it's my phone. When I pull it out of my pocket, I find a group message from Mibs and Lally and Gordon, asking if I want to meet them tonight at our coffee place, Quirky Perks. I get an idea.

"Joey, can I have your phone number?" He's a little surprised when I tell him, "I have some friends I want to introduce you to, if you'd like." We exchange numbers. Then he takes Tess's bag and holds the car door open for her, as if he were her boyfriend.

As I watch Tess drive away from me in a big old truck, sitting next to a boy, the wind picks up a little and it starts to snow.

Chapter Twenty-Eight

... A YEAR LATER...

Tess.

It's supposed to snow tonight. A blizzard, which will shut down the trains and the taxis. A storm like New York hasn't seen in years. I don't see Soph before. Not because there's a rule against it, but because I'm stuck in my own schedule—my pass to leave for the City doesn't start until noon, and by the time I take the bus across town and get to where I'm supposed to be, she's already behind a door, preparing. She calls me while they're doing her hair.

"This is ridiculous, Tess," she grumbles. "My hair is pulled back so tight I can't close my mouth. The damn comb is practically nailed into my skull. And wait 'til you see the red lipstick. I look like this year's queen of the flamenco dancers."

"You look so beautiful," I tell her.

That makes her laugh. "You can't even see me!"

I tell her, "I don't need to."

"I can't believe you talked me into this... this *tradition*. I should be hanging on the wall in a gallery at the Prado."

I chuckle. "'The most significant of tradition...'"

"I know, I know, 'Survives and blooms through endless revision.' What was I thinking? Right now, I just feel like something from the seventeenth century. I am not the least bit revised."

"You are, though."

And then she has to go, to finish getting ready. I know all I have to do now is wait. I wait and wait and wait, and, finally it's time to adjust my jacket and my gloves. I follow the directions to where the chaperones tell me to stand. I hand the little card to a lady standing by a microphone behind the curtains, announcing the debutantes.

She looks at me with her eyebrows raised, then inspects the card again. She's confused. "Is this right?" she asks me. "Do you realize you're escorting…"

"A girl," I say, and I don't so much as blink, just stand as though I was at attention in front of her. "I'm escorting my girlfriend, Sophronia Borbón del Alcazar. I'm West Point Cadet Tess Desmarais, First Year, ma'am. As you know, West Point had a long tradition of providing escorts for the young ladies who are first presented at this ball until very recently. My First Captain, ma'am—she's a woman, too—granted me special leave to attend. I guess we're starting a new tradition."

The woman blinks at me and looks back at the card. She clearly has no idea what to say. So I add, "And yes, I know she's a girl. Respectfully, ma'am, she knows I'm one too."

Then Soph is next to me. She says my name, and I can barely breathe because I was right: She's beautiful with her long black hair piled on her head under her family's comb, the lace falling behind her. She is wearing the most elegant, full-skirted, heavy white ball gown I've ever seen. The lace of her skirt matches her mantilla. The announcer reads her name and mine, and I put out my arm for her to take. We walk out into bright lights and flashbulbs and applause.

Later, after she dances with her father and we eat prime rib with a bunch of other girls and their escorts, Soph sneaks me out to one of the hotel balconies. She giggles that glittery laugh I still love, and tries to pull me into her white fur wrap for a hug. But I won't let her, because the escorts were warned against PDA and, if I get in trouble here, I won't be allowed off campus again until Memorial Day. I stand right next to her, though, and hold her hands, which are covered in opera-length white gloves. She apologizes.

"I know you used to watch Disney movies and always wanted to dress up in the ball gown. I'm sorry they made me wear it instead," she says.

"I what?" I say, not understanding her. Then I remember the talk we had back at the conference. "Silly," I tell her, "when I said I used to watch those movies and imagine being at a ball with the music and the ball gown, it was never me wearing it."

"It wasn't?"

She's surprised, and I laugh out loud at her, but there's no bite to it. "I'm a girl who likes girls, Soph. I was always watching the princesses in their ball gowns because I wanted to *dance* with them. Not because I wanted to *dress* like them." She laughs with me, and we look out across the city at all the lit-up buildings. I'm not sure I could ever live here; the city is so crowded. But I'm glad to be here with Soph tonight.

"Is your family all right with you being here?" she asks gently.

"They will be," I say. Maybe I'm starting to believe it. "But Joey texted from Boston. He found a new job, one that pays better, and Orly is coming up in March, right?"

"Yes," she says. We both stop talking.

We can hear the dance music and the sounds of clinking crystal and silverware and conversation coming through the glass doors. Out here the night is dark, despite the city lights. Soph shivers in her wrap. We stand together, enduring the cold. Neither of us wants to go back inside.

I kiss her, even though I'm breaking the rules. She's too beautiful not to kiss tonight, and I know I'll regret it forever if I don't.

"Will you dance with me now?" I ask, because we have to rejoin the party. "I want to experience the full Sophronian tradition of a debutante ball. It may be my only chance."

When she smiles and gives me her hand, snow starts to drift down out of the night sky like a blessing on both of us.

✳ ✳ ✳

From the Fan Fiction Unbound Archive,
posted by conTessaofthecastle and Debutaunt:

Daphne and Astoria stood in the wooded clearing, a ring of witches surrounding them. Today they were sharing the magic they had acquired with their new coven. Astoria's royal blue cape fluttered softly in the breeze. Her hair, braided with matching blue ribbons, glinted auburn in the sunlight. Daphne couldn't look away. Her own soft gold cape pooled around her ankles. Daphne's mind wandered to the weeks before: Astoria fetching wood for the fire, hunched over the wooden table as she studied the spell book, lying close in the dark of their bed each night. Astoria's voice had whispered spells in the dark each night, lulling Daphne to sleep with magic. They had worked and practiced and talked. And they had finally created the enchantment that would bind them to each other and to their own coven.

Adder's fork and carrot nose,
Tiny shoes on porcelain toes,
Silver moon, fav'rable Venus.
We need none of it between us.

Bat's wool, dog's tongue, newt's right eye,
Laws of nature we defy.
Heaven's blessings, absent Uranus,
We need neither to sustain us.

Demons, gorgons to placate.
Better angels susurrate.
Garland of roses to link us,
Fragrance of ash forever syncs us.

My heart, your heart, they demand,
"Love each other," their command.
Make no sacrifice too tragic—
Love becomes our strongest magic.

As bright sun wound its way through the spring leaves on the trees towering overhead, Daphne reached for Astoria's hand. "How shall we proceed?" she asked with a smile. Astoria looked back at her with a wide-eyed happiness that drove every other thought from Daphne's mind and said, again, "Together."

Acknowledgments

First, and foremost, we acknowledge our wonderful, supportive, patient families: Dan, Giancarlo, Nicholas, and Paul. Thank you for giving us time and space to write and for putting up with us! Additional thanks to Nicholas and Paul for always texting back when we had a question about what word to use.

Second, we are indebted to Interlude Press for taking on a pair of novice authors. Thank you to Annie Harper, for advocating for *Snowsisters* and editing the various drafts and improving them at every stage. CB Messer's cover is amazing and distinct—even better than we hoped. Candy Miller shared her extensive marketing talents, and we hope some rubbed off. All three have been very kind to us along the way, and we appreciate it.

Several talented women helped us form Soph, Tess, and Orly and their interactions at the Young Women's Writing Conference. June Amelia Rose suggested scenes and plot twists which we gratefully incorporated. Ashley Lauren Rogers provided solid and thoughtful insight. Micaela Slotin and Jen Stacey both gave early input and let us know where we needed to change course. Heidi Seary read several drafts and offered valuable feedback.

We are indebted to authors Sarah Weeks and Jodi Picoult, both bestselling, talented writers who have offered remarkably kind, generous support and assistance along the way. We are grateful to Anna Wilinsky for letting us use her experiences at a writing conference and to Taylor Carroll for teaching us about dairy cows.

The Wakefield Writing Group believed in Soph and Tess and gave us a valuable first critique. Bethel Saler, Lori Berhon, Elizabeth Santis, Parrish Finn, Mary Ann Oehlerking, Louis Biancone, Joan Robins, Sharis Pozen, Shelly Sawyer, Charlotte Wilinsky, Robin Kall, Joanna Henderson, Christine Turner, Holly Eaves, and others told us we could do it and believed it. We can't tell you how much that means.

And thank *you* for reading *Snowsisters*.

—Tom Wilinsky & Jen Sternick

About the Authors

WE'RE TOM AND JEN. WE met in high school and started a conversation which, years later, is ongoing.

About Tom: Tom lives in New York with his partner and the world's most beloved orange tabby cat, Newky. He's an attorney who likes cold weather, anything with zombies in it, and old cars. Never has he ever: been picked first for a team in Phys. Ed, used a selfie stick, gotten Jen to watch an episode of South Park.

About Jen: Jen lives in Rhode Island with her husband, two sons, and a cranky, seven-toed cat named Sassy. She's a former criminal prosecutor who still works in government. She likes live theater and traveling to places she's never been and she admits to being mildly addicted to Twitter. Never has she ever: left the last deviled egg on a plate, been able to sing the theme song from The Big Bang Theory, convinced Tom to read a self-help book.

About Never Have I Ever Books: We're both avid readers and share books, recipes, music, and strong opinions. As Never Have I Ever Books on Tumblr, Twitter, Instagram, and Facebook, we follow, write, and review YA LGBTQIAP+ fiction, fan fiction, and popular media.

an imprint of interlude **press**

@duet**books**

Twitter | Tumblr

For a reader's guide to **Snowsisters** *and
book club prompts, please visit duetbooks.com.*

also from **duet.**

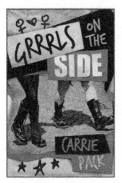

Grrrls on the Side by Carrie Pack

The year is 1994, and alternative is in, except for high schooler Tabitha Denton. Uninterested in boys, lonely, and sidelined by former friends, she finds her escape in a punk concert zine: an ad for a Riot Grrrl meet-up. There, Tabitha discovers herself, love, and how to stand up for what's right.

ISBN (print) 978-1-945053-21-4 | (eBook) 978-1-945053-37-5

The Seafarer's Kiss by Julia Ember

Mermaid Ersel rescues the maiden Ragna and learns the life she wants is above the sea. Desperate, Ersel makes a deal with Loki but the outcome is not what she expects. To fix her mistakes and be reunited with Ragna, Ersel must now outsmart the God of Lies.

ISBN (print) 978-1-945053-20-7 | (eBook) 978-1-945053-34-4

Not Your Sidekick by C.B. Lee

Welcome to Andover, where superpowers are common— but not for Jessica Tran. Despite her heroic lineage, Jess is resigned to a life without superpowers when an internship for Andover's resident super villain allows her to work alongside her longtime crush Abby and helps her unravel a plot larger than heroes and villains altogether.

ISBN (print) 978-1-945053-03-0 | (eBook) 978-1-945053-04-7

CPSIA information can be obtained
at www.ICGtesting.com
Printed in the USA
LVOW03s2318040218
565301LV00001B/74/P